THE MAP MAKER

THE
MAP
MAKER

Matthew J. Krengel

NORTH STAR PRESS OF ST. CLOUD, INC.
Saint Cloud, Minnesota

First Edition: September 2012

Printed in the United States of America

Published by
North Star Press of St. Cloud, Inc.
P.O. Box 451
St. Cloud, Minnesota 56302

www.northstarpress.com

THE MAP MAKER

PROLOGUE
Sixteen years ago in another place . . .

I T'S HAPPENED," a voice said, trying to remain calm despite the excitement and a bit of fear that was present. "The one we seek has been born somewhere."

"What do we do?"

The voice that spoke was nervous, and it cracked and grated on the ears of the few people still attending the small gathering. All of those in attendance were nervous. These days being caught in certain company was the same as signing a death warrant from the Adherents. The religious fervor of the group drove it to commit acts that many viewed as worse than extreme, but those who thought that kept their thoughts to themselves lest they be the next targets.

"I'm going across soon, and I'm taking our map with me," the leader of their small group said. His voice was much calmer but even it displayed more than a bit of nervous energy. This was their last desperate chance to find someone with the ability to bring the scattered groups together under one standard of defiance against the might of the Temple of the Adherency.

"But if you take it there . . . I mean what if one of *them* gets it? You could be stranded there forever." A clamor of questions bombarded the short leader of the group. He shook his head at them.

"Wouldn't it be worse if it stayed here and was captured? Besides we've searched our world for almost a hundred years and haven't found a single mapmaker with the skills we require. There hardly exists the ability to create maps at all any

N
W ◄ 1 ► E
S

more on this side of the Divide. It's as though the skill is fading from our world. Maybe we have been searching in the wrong world," the leader replied. He looked around and tried to meet each of their eyes, he did his best to impart a bit of his strength into each of them but sadly he had little left to give.

"But none of them even believes in us anymore," another voice hissed from the floor. "I mean that's why our worlds were separated. Right? The majority of humans wanted nothing to do with us. We're too strange to them . . . our forms are too different for their minds to comprehend anymore."

"It matters little," the leader said again, this time his voice much more forceful. "At the rate the Adherents are gaining artifacts and the power they contain, they will soon be able to affect things in both worlds. It's more than just the maps and the power they represent. Remember that. When the Divide was created, our world was the storage place for *thousands* of items of immense power. Anything the ancients deemed as magical or out of place in the mundane world was sent here, believing that they would be safe. And for a long time they were. But now the Adherents are nearing that tipping point when they'll begin fomenting chaos across the Divide. That will weaken it. If they weaken it enough, it might be brought down. And that, my dear friends . . . that could destroy both our worlds." He sighed, emotion working his face. Then his expression firmed, and he continued. "Besides, I believe that the one we seek has been born on the *other* side of the Divide. We can't risk waiting. Not with the Adherents moving so quickly. It'll take time to prepare the crossing so it will go unnoticed, but I must . . . absolutely *must* cross over and attempt to find that one."

A sudden round of muttering made all of those in attendance look about nervously, hoping no one had heard their words. The Adherents had so many eyes and ears in so many places. Those who forgot that important fact generally ended up on a slave ship headed out to the northern mines. All present knew those sent to the north rarely returned except as worn out husks of their former selves.

"Listen, all of you," the leader said in a hushed whisper that carried the weight of magic in his voice. "I want you all to return to your lives. Harbor what hope you can. Share our words carefully but take no chances. I'll be gone for some time, but when I return it'll be with one who has the power to begin undoing what Cain and his Adherents have done to our world. Hold that hope. Now go before we're betrayed."

They left the house slowly, never more than two at a time and in different directions than where they lived. Hushed words of encouragement had followed people to the door, and the leader had nodded and tried hard to look certain, but when he was finally alone, he slumped into his chair and rested his head wearily in his hands. Despair dogged the heels of any hope he had.

The tiny fire he kept burning in his hearth provided only the smallest amount of light to his cottage on the edge of the rocky cliffs overlooking the great northern port city of Duluth. Great Duluth with its library and center of learning was meant to be the last bastion of civilization in the wilds of the northwest but now it had become a stronghold of fanaticism.

Why do they all have to look to me for guidance? he wondered. He was tired. He would have accepted just going quietly to his rest. If left up to him, he'd step out of the focus, enjoy the gentle retirement of walking barefoot in his garden, feeling the gritty soil between his toes, and stopping to smell the fragrance of the leaves of a hundred different spices as they grew in swirls and patterns. But he could not.

Being leader was what had come to him, what he now must do. But it took so much energy. When he finally felt he could move again, he rose and walked about his small cottage on the edge of the forest. High above the great Lake Superior, he could look down as the great iron ships of the Adherents rode the waves into port to take on loads of raw iron and often slaves captured in the wilds. Hundreds of frightened beings gathered from their homes deep in the forests were sent south to work in the factories that belched smoke and fouled the air and the ground around them or, worse, sent north to the mines. Those hapless ones found themselves bound in iron and forced deep under the ground never to see the light of day again. The rate at which the Adherents were spreading poison across the world made him shake his head in sorrow and depair.

But when hundreds of individuals had searched their world long and hard and come up empty, he had looked across the Divide for the special one. But that effort was exhausting. It had taken him days to recover. Still he had found reason to be encouraged. The people living on the other side had more sense than to spew out as much poison into their world as the Adherents dumped into theirs.

He stood at the small window in his cottage that looked down at the port of Duluth and the great bridge that connected the vast forested hills of Wiscon to Duluth. Even those forests were falling now to the Adherents as hundreds of men with iron axes felled trees. At such a rate, within a few years they would have deforested the entire area for miles in all directions. He could close his eyes and imagine the first row of brown hills. It saddened him. Worse, though, was the threat that without their covering of trees the hills fell under the onslaught of the rain. Muddy water filled the few rivers that crossed the area. Fish choked and died in the oxygen-depleted waters and floated away, fouling the rivers even more with their carcasses.

"Now is not the time for such thoughts," the leader muttered to himself sternly. He jerked the curtain shut and turned away from the destruction. He had much work to do. He fastened his front door against the occasional visitor, and then banked the fire for the night. At the back of his cottage stood a small bookshelf, empty of course since books were banned outside of the Temple of Adherency. Still it served him well as storage space for small items he found useful—a bag of spices, a few round bits of northern agates collected before such activities were banned. But he had not gone to the shelves to examine his treasures. Ignoring the items he worked the hidden latch so that the bookcase swung to the side. A set of stairs stretched down into the ground into darkness. He lit a torch and descended the steps. On cue, the shelf swung back into place and the latch clicked.

The torch cast a flickering circle of light around his feet. Down nearly a hundred steps he trudged until the stairs stopped before another door. When he swung the portal open, he was greeted with a bit of light. He dipped his torch into a waiting bucket of water. It extinguised with a hiss.

The doused torch was set to the side to dry, and he turned to his workshop. Even under the weight of his concerns and in the face of his physical exhaustion, he had to smile. Here he was safe. Protected by what magics he could still work without drawing attention, here he could work without fear of interruption. He turned in a slow circle, cataloguing everything in in the cluttered space, making sure that nothing had been moved—a small but necessary caution. Not even the Adherents with their vast network of spies could know of this place, not if he was to accomplish his greatest work ever. Wooden shelves lined the walls and a single fire fed with bits of coal kept the workplace warm, while smokeless lights kept it well lit. His tables were filled with glass beakers and clay jars filled with exotic items—bits of plants and stones, curious twisted roots, small bags filled with minerals. A small forge built into the corner was ready for him to bring his hammer and tongs over and finish his work. But his real treasure was his collection of books, hundreds of them. They filled his shelves in carefully ranked rows and rough piles. In these books he had the knowledge that many thought was lost to his world.

The Adherents would kill to lay their hands on what was stored in his workroom. Books contained vast knowledge and it could be passed to anyone who wished to learn. He had books on herbs that described potions that would heal and those that would kill, volumes that told how to interact with the thousands of species of mortal beings that lived and died on this world. Ancient books showed the making of maps and the construction of the tools of power that had made lives of mortals easier for a millennium before the Divide was put in place. His books had been rescued from the great library before the horrible night so many years ago when knowledge ended in huge bonfires.

"That's how it started," the leader muttered with conviction, and he started forward into his laboratory. "They started by burning books." Few were old enough to have seen this even, but he still remembered. The image was still sharp in his mind. Cain and his Adherents had arrived at the city gates. Smiling and laughing and glib of tongue, the charismatic leader of the Adherents quickly became the most popular person in the port city. He passed out gifts and preached the words of his religion to anyone who would listen, spreading what he called a better way of life to the masses. Conversions took place quickly. Soon more than half the city claimed allegiance to Cain. Only then had things begun to change, starting with unexplained disappearances. Those who asked after the missing soon went missing themselves. People stopped asking.

Then rumors spread that the city was at danger from violent criminals living in the forests. After a few bloody raids, the people begged Cain to protect them. Slowly at first and with many promises he finally agreed. Within two weeks the first of the great iron ships docked and disgorged hundreds of men in the black-and-red uniforms. Adherency had arrived in force. The people began to wonder who were worse: the protectors or the raiders. Then the bonfires had been lit and the library of Duluth sacked of its treasures, not for the benefit of foreign conquerers, but for destruction.

Tears crept into his eyes and slid into the lines of his ancient face as he remembered the day when he nearly died ferreting out what tomes he could as the fires crept across the building.

He walked to his workbench and looked down at the half completed compass that had occupied his mind and effort for untold months. It was to be his greatest work. A device of great power, the compass would give its wielder the ability to use any map, not just those few still containing power from when the Divide was put in place. But should this compass fall into the wrong hands, it would doom both worlds. And the leader had no assurance that even the world he had glimpsed through the divide could stand against Cain and his Adherents.

Still he dared not stop, even with the dangers. He knew a map maker with the right skills had been born, and he knew a runner who would work with the cartographer was also alive. That was the salvation he risked all to reach. He just needed to find him or her. He had to finish his compass before Cain's spies found him, and then he had to cross over and begin his search.

CHAPTER ONE
Late Again

CLICK
Click
The channels flipped by Jane's eyes as her fingers flashed at the remote's tiny buttons in a desperate attempt to banish the boredom that threatened to take her sanity. It was seven in the evening, and already her mom was two hours late getting home from work. She'd promised no more late nights, but that was another promise broken before Jane had even finished school for the year. Sitting on the coffee table near Jane's feet were the two tickets to Orchestra Hall, now worthless considering the concert started an hour ago.

"Usual for a Friday," Jane muttered. "If she's still even at work and not over at Derek's house." Her mom's newest boyfriend drove her nuts with his overpowered motorcycle and the way he wore his hair, drawn back into a pony tail. He was her mom's usual desperate attempt to shake off the mundane existence of an accountant with a fast motorcycle and a thinning head of hair grown out into a pony tail.

She grabbed her cell phone off the couch next to her and flipped to her favorites, looking at the little smiling image of her mom that stared back at her. Just the second week of summer break and what was she doing? Sitting at home waiting for her mother.

After her parents divorced, Jane spent most of her time with her mother, but now with summer it was time for her annual pilgrimage to her grandparents' house. That was the highlight of her summer. She could be herself away from the demands of the track coach at school and her mom constantly bugging her about her grades.

A sound out in the hallway brought her to her feet. She started toward the door. Then she heard Max bellow and she stopped. Max lived at the end of the hall. One of the joys of living on the tenth floor was that only so many people could afford to live this high in the air.

She walked over to the patio door and stepped out onto the wide concrete porch that filled in this side of the spacious condominium. The sun was dipping dangerously low in the sky. She leaned on the railing watching the traffic fill Interstate 94 in the distance. Already bumper to bumper out there. She could see an accident pulled off to the side of the freeway where the slowdown began. Blue and red lights whirled. Probably why her mom was running late, but she was unwilling to cut her any slack.

Ring. Ring.

Jane fumbled with her iPhone, then finally got it out of her pocket and answered the call.

"Jane," her mother's voice came through the plastic case. "Are you there?" She sounded frustrated and angry.

"Hi, mom," Jane said. She fiddled with the handle on the railing as she waited for the answer. In the background she could hear the car radio playing and the honk of angry drivers. Obviously she was stuck in traffic.

"I'm sorry, Jane," her mother started. "I know the tickets were for six, but I couldn't get out."

"Where are you?"

"Where do you think I am?" her mother laughed but there was little humor in her voice. "I'm stuck in traffic about half a mile from home. You can probably see me from the balcony. I should just leave the car here and walk home."

"It might be faster," Jane replied. She squinted and searched the row of cars until she spotted her mother's red Acura about twenty cars back from the accident. "Got you. You're almost to the accident. Maybe the traffic will pick up after that." She tried to see the end of the line of vehicles, but it disappeared around a bend in the freeway out of her sight.

"Hope so. I was hoping to spend a little time with you this evening."

"Well, I was hoping to see you too," Jane muttered crossly.

"Don't get rude with me. I didn't ask to work late today."

Jane pulled the phone away from ear as her mom launched into a lecture. She turned away from the balcony railing, walked back into the living room and flopped back down on the couch. She propped her feet up on the glass coffee table. A bottle of red nail polish sat next to the remote. She tucked the phone back up to her ear just in time to hear the last of the lecture and began touching up the polish on her toenails.

"Good. I'm past the accident, I'm going to pick up some food. I'll be home in a couple minutes. See you soon."

"See you soon," Jane parroted, then she flipped the phone down on the couch and turned the volume back up on the TV. She could see her reflection in the flat screen and noticed idly that her blond hair matched the reporter's perfectly. Suddenly she sat up and turned the volume up even more.

"Odd happenings today in the Duluth area. What appears to be a rogue wave struck shore, damaging ships and property along the shores of Lake Superior. Eye witnesses said the water briefly flooded over into Canal Park and sent people scrambling for higher ground. The Coast Guard confirmed that the water did come over into the park for a time and that they recorded an odd pattern of waves over the last days but nothing this substantial."

N

W — 10 — E

S

Jane sat up a bit straighter and grabbed her phone. She pulled up her grandpa's number and hit the call button. The phone rang six times before a gruff voice answered and she smiled to herself. He sounded like an old bear.

"Grandpa," Jane said excitedly. Her friends made fun of her every year when summer break came and she began talking about her annual visit to her grandparents. It seemed so boring to them, her days spent playing Scrabble with her grandma and walking the wooded trails around Duluth with her grandpa. Simple activities and time to herself away from the rat race of the Cities—the honking horns, the bumper-to-bumper traffic. It seemed odd to be needing time away when she was mad at her mom for not being home, but that was different. "I heard that something happened down on the lake."

"Oh, ya. Buncha tourists got all worked up about a high wave or something," Grandpa Arnie muttered in his rough voice. "Nuthin' to worry about, girl. Are you still coming this weekend?"

The question in his voice was obvious. She smiled, feeling his impatience as he waited for her to answer. She knew he looked forward to having someone to walk with now that grandma was confined to the house.

"Wouldn't miss it for the world, Grandpa. You know that," Jane said as she shifted the phone on her shoulder to a more comfortable position. They chatted a few minutes until Jane heard the key moving in the front door. "Gotta go, Grandpa. Mom's home. See you soon."

"Okay. Yes, see you soon, Jany."

She flipped the television off and walked to the front door. Her mother was setting packages inside the door. "What did you get?" Jane asked.

"Chinese."

"Ooo, my favorite. Did you get eggrolls?" Jane asked as she started rummaging through the containers.

"Of course."

She gave her mom a quick hug and took the bags of food into the kitchen area. As annoying as her mom could be, Jane still loved her, and they got along well most of the time.

"Want to watch a movie while we eat?"

"Sure," Jane said. "Which one?"

"I don't care. You pick."

"*Twilight*?" Jane asked.

"Fine," Her mother called out from the back bedroom.

A few minutes later they were sitting on the leather sofa with the food spread out on the coffee table before them. Both of them were dressed in sweats and sweaters. They were much alike, often confused for sisters, though Jane could easily see the laugh lines on her mother's face. As the movie started, Jane looked nervously at her mom, considering asking—her mom had talked a few times of not letting her go north this summer.

"What is it?" her mother asked finally.

"I talked to Grandpa today," Jane said. "He wanted to make sure I was still coming."

"I hardly get to see you anymore. Can't you stop growing up just for a few years?"

"Mom, please," Jane begged. She hated stooping to begging but this was her only chance to get away. Four weeks with her grandparents, who would do anything she asked, eat anywhere she wanted to eat, and Grandpa would shuttle her anywhere she wanted to go to take pictures. "Grandpa's so looking forward to my coming . So is Grandma."

"I'm just kidding. Yes, you're still going if you want too."

Jane squealed and wrapped a great hug around her mom, almost spilling half the food in the process.

"All right then. Food and movie. Then I need to get some sleep. We have two days together before I have to take you to the train station. After that it's back into work and try and catch up last quarter's numbers."

"When you retire that place is going to be lost," Jane said as she settled back to watch Edward and Bella.

"Yeah, well until then I'm going to take what work I can get and be glad I still have a job. They laid off three more in our department alone last month."

"Anything else interesting happen?"

"Well, yes, some weird-looking bum was escorted out of the building by security. He was asking for me, they said. They had a picture of him, but I have never seen him before in my life. Shortest little guy I have ever seen who wasn't a midget and wearing the oddest looking bowler hat. Security said he kept going on about maps and compasses. I think they were going to call the police and see if St Peter's was missing a patient."

"Huh?" Jane replied. She pulled an egg roll from the container and juggled it momentarily as she blew on her fingers trying not to burn herself. Whatever else her mom was saying was lost on her as Bella accused Edward of being a vampire.

CHAPTER TWO
Here Be Dragons

"MOM, CAN WE GO DOWN to the science museum?" Jane asked as she stepped out of the bathroom and walked down to her room. Thankfully the walk was short, and she was off the cold tile in the hallway and onto the carpet of her room quickly. She left the door ajar so she could hear the reply as she dressed.

"Why? What new exhibits do they have?"

Jane rolled her eyes. Her mom knew full well that the Smithsonian's traveling map collection was being displayed. Once more it irritated her that she had to hide her interest from most of her friends at school. The last thing she needed was for them to hear how she had to convince her mom to take her down to the museum to see some old maps. "Mom."

"I'm kidding," her mother called back. "Let's get breakfast done, and then we can drive down there for the morning. Are you bringing your camera with?"

Good thought. Jane grabbed her Canon and her sketch book along with an assortment of pencils and pens and slid them into a shoulder bag that would hide them well enough if they ran into anyone she knew.

"Yes," Jane said as she entered the kitchen area of their apartment. "And my sketch book."

"I still remember last year when you dragged me down there to see the Dead Sea Scrolls," her mother complained. "I'm not staying there all day again just so you can draw a picture of every single thing. Keep that in mind."

"I promise," Jane said. "But Mr. Conners said that if I did a report on the map exhibit, he'd bump my history grade from a *B* to an *A*."

"By all means then," her mother said as she set down a bowl of oatmeal on the counter and poured a cup of orange juice. "I still can't believe you got a *B* in history. It's always been one of your favorite subjects."

"Well, Erin Thompson said it was pointless, and she keeps making fun of the teacher. It's really hard to concentrate with all that drama," Jane finished lamely. She shrugged and smiled, "Don't wind up the grades-are-important lecture. I know, Mom. I know my grades are going to affect how much financial aid I can get and what schools will accept me."

"That's the guts of my lecture, so I'll let it go," her mother said. "Come on. Eat up, and we'll drive down there to improve your chances of getting into college. It's a perfect day out though. I want to stop by the park on the way home and go running. Want to come along for the run?"

"Sure," Jane returned to her room for her work out bag. Twenty minutes later they were zooming along I-94 towards downtown St Paul. They exited south onto Jackson Street and drove until they reached Kellogg Boulevard. Coming from this direction they could park in the sunshine near the museum and walk the last few blocks rather than park in the dungeon of a parking garage. The mighty Mississippi flowed below them, just beginning its march through the continent.

Her mom had paid the membership fee at the Science Museum at the beginning of the year, and so they waved their passes and entered unchallenged into the vast collection of exhibits and displays. There were few visitors about the entry, and Jane hoped it would remain that way at least until they were gone. She hated fighting through hundreds of ten year olds at every display case, but the parents with toddlers in strollers were even worse.

"Isn't it amazing," Jane muttered as she stood staring down at the copper globe listed as the Lenox Globe on loan from the New York Public Library. "Look, it says despite popular myth this is the only ancient map that actually contains the phrase 'Here be dragons.' Why would they say that right on a globe?" The globe was intricately carved and in amazing shape. It rested in a display case next to a modern replica that had been labeled in English. This one was out in the open for people to see and touch.

"I don't know." Her mom said as she looked down at the globe. "Maybe it expressed a fear of the unknown. It was made over five hundred years ago, so who knows what they thought back then."

"Maybe a dragon lived there," a voice rasped behind her.

Jane was startled. She looked up and her eyebrows nearly disappeared into her hair. The man was short, she figured just over half of her height but his body seemed to be proportioned normally, just a bit thick. He had a scruffy beard that, instead of looking creepy, made him seem jolly, and he wore the oddest combination of clothing she had ever seen. Jane looked over at her mom, but she had been drawn to a case across the hall and was not paying any attention.

"Dragons don't exist," Jane pointed out haughtily. She smirked and looked down at the little man as she pulled the cover off her camera and prepared to snap a picture of the globe. "Everyone knows that."

"How do you know that?" he asked as he stood on his toes and looked at the globe contained inside the case. A smile creased his lined face. "I remember when he carved those words," the little man whispered softly.

"Because," Jane repeated. "Everyone knows that." She rolled her eyes. Clearly the little man was not all there in the head. Jane stepped to the other side of the case.

"'Everyone knows,'" the little man said in a mocking voice. "I know a few dragons that would love to argue that point with you."

"What . . . ?" Jane muttered as her eyebrows scrunched up in confusion.

"This beautiful globe is filled with power from a day when amazing things took place every day," the little man muttered more to himself than to her. "I don't doubt for a moment that the cartographer who created this masterpiece was trying to warn people that there was a dragon living in that area."

"What?" Jane exclaimed. She rolled her eyes to the ceiling and shook her head. "Look . . . !" She said, ready to confront him, but she stopped. The little man was gone.

"What was that Jane?" her mom asked. She was walking back from the far side of the hallway and looked at her questioningly.

"Nothing," Jane muttered. "I think I spent too much time inside this summer so far." She leaned over and looked at the etchings on the globe more closely, examining the tiny emblem carved in the surface from just above the protective glass shield.

There was an image of a dragon etched into the metal. Jane stared at it in fascination. Suddenly the tiny image seemed to turn and look at her from behind the glass. She gasped and jumped back, startling her mother.

"What is it?" her mom said as she stepped back.

"Nothing," Jane muttered. "I think I stared at it too long." She raised her camera and snapped a photo of the whole globe and then narrowed down and snapped a photo of the dragon itself.

They continued walking along the line of displays. The cases held exhibits from across the globe. Near the end of the line they saw five maps from the seventeenth and eighteenth century that encompassed the Great Lakes.

"Hey, look, they have Lake Superior on these," Jane pointed out. "These are the ones Mr. Conners wanted a report on. "Look, here's one made in 1755 by someone named D'Anville." She took several photos of the map before leaning closer to the case to examine it.

Suddenly she felt as if someone watched her. She glanced about. Standing in the corner was that small oddly dressed man. He nodded at her when their eyes met, and then turned and walked into the next room. She turned back to the map and began sketching it as quickly as she could. When she reached the top left side of the map, she started drawing in the beaver depicted on it, when suddenly the animal turned its head and looked at her. This time Jane dropped her pencil and stared in shock. *That's not possible*, she repeated to herself over and over.

"What happened?" her mom asked from where she was sitting on a bench near the opposite wall. She was fiddling with her phone but looked up for a moment to see what Jane was doing.

"Nothing, I dropped my pencil," Jane muttered over her shoulder. She leaned over and picked up the charcoal pencil and finished her sketch before moving on to the last couple maps. All of them were drawn by Frenchmen and all were from before the eighteen hundreds so she wrote down what information she could and then followed her mom out towards the exit.

"There he is again," her mom said suddenly. She pointed towards the door leading back out to the street and came to a sudden halt.

Jane followed to where her mom was pointing and noticed that the short man was sitting quietly near the exit. His eyes seemed to be glued to her. They left the building and as Jane stepped out of the exit door she looked at the little man one more time. This time he smiled at her hesitantly and then she was gone out the door. *What a strange little man.*

They walked slowly back to where the car was parked, enjoying the sun and warmth that was hard to count on in Minnesota so early in the summer. The sky was filled with fluffy clouds that moved ponderously across the ocean of blue on a timetable all their own.

"Let's go for that run," her mom said when they arrived at the Lillydale Park.

Jane wanted nothing to do with running at the moment but she figured it might help relieve the apprehension she was feeling, so she nodded and slipped her running shoes on. They left the car parked and began jogging along the paved trail. Slowly the stress that had built up over the morning slipped away, leaving her loose and relaxed. The trail wandered the banks of the river for a few miles in each direction and they enjoyed watching the people who had gathered to eat lunches and fly kites in the warmth. They were on their way back from the end of their circuit when suddenly her mom said suddenly, "What a weird-looking character."

Jane looked to where she was pointing and had to agree. Standing in the shadow of a mighty oak tree near the river was a man wear a black robe. Across his chest was a red medallion, and he stared at them with open hostility. His face was thin and there were pock marks across his features. His eyes were black and a sneer made his face seem sinister.

"I'm glad plenty of people are around because he gives me the creeps," Jane muttered. She looked the other way and noticed a police cruiser parked near the running trail. She nodded towards the officer. "I think we should have the police check him out," whispered to her mom. She looked back to the place where the robed person had stood. No one was there. He had managed to disappear faster than she would have thought anyone could.

CHAPTER THREE
Trains and Strangers

S UNDAY CAME WITH A BRILLIANT burst of sunshine, but then the sky quickly turned gray as storm clouds swept off the plains to the west. Jane stumbled out of bed at around nine and went in search of food, her hair was frazzled and she wrapped herself in a thick robe as she followed the smells coming from the kitchen.

"Ah, you're up. Good."

"Hmm, that smells good," Jane said as she leaned over the stove and took stock of what her mom was cooking. Eggs, bacon, and a tray of biscuits. Her mouth watered and she looked about for a plate.

"Go clean up quick and then we can eat. Besides it'll take a few more minutes for me to finish this." Her mom shooed her back out of the kitchen with her oven mitt.

"Fine," Jane muttered. But she snagged a piece of bacon from the edge of the pan and fled to the bathroom before her mom could stop her.

They ate a quiet breakfast, focusing on the great food. When they finished and the kitchen was clean, Jane felt ready to face the train ride north. As her mom finished drying the last of the plates, Jane retrieved her suitcase from the corner of her bedroom. She had packed the night before. All that remained was to grab her camera case.

Jane and her mom walked to the garage in the basement of their building. As Jane stuffed her suitcase into the trunk, her mom started the car. The closest Amtrak station was in St.

N

W ←(21)→ E

S

Paul, which was a bit of a ride. Jane tossed her backpack in the back seat and slid into the passenger seat, found a comfortable position and slid her earphones on. She was half way through the first song when she noticed her mom was talking to her.

They had hardly pulled out of the driveway when her mom waved a hand in front of her face. Jane jumped and said, "Huh?"

"Can you turn that thing off for a minute so we can talk?"

Guiltily Jane turned the volume down and tried to listen.

"Teach grandpa how to use his Ipad while you're there."

"What?" Jane muttered. She removed the earphones and waited for her mom to continue.

Rolling her eyes, her mom repeated herself. "Grandpa bought himself an Ipad a couple of weeks ago so he can talk to your aunt in Hawaii. Teach him how to use it while you're there."

"Oh, sure that'll be easy. I can set up Skype and make sure it works for him."

"Easy for you, yes, but not so easy for a seventy-three-year old who's never even owned a cell phone before last year."

"I'll get it all set up for him, mom," Jane reassured her.

They were nearing the train station, and Jane was feeling a little apprehension about leaving. She'd miss her mom even if she was looking forward to time with her grandparents. As they pulled into the parking lot, she gathered up her camera and phone and tucked them into her backpack. Her mom found a parking spot near the entrance. Once they were inside the building Jane set her luggage down near the loading area and turned to her mom. There was a mist of tears already in her mom's eyes.

"Oh, mom, don't cry," Jane muttered. "I've made this trip like eight times."

"Yes, but normally your sister'd be with you."

That brought a mist of tears to Jane's eyes as well. She had done her best to keep it out of her head that this would be her first summer without her big sister. Jackie had disappeared almost a year ago without a trace. After an exhaustive search of the area that lasted almost four months, the police had called off the search. Jackie's disappearance had caused other problems. Her parents started fighting, and Jane thought it was a blame thing. A few months later her parents had divorced, and Jane's father moved back to Colorado where his family lived.

Jackie had disappeared without a trace—no note, no hint, no nothing. Her friends had been clueless. Worse, she had told Jane nothing of her plans, and the two of them had been close. One moment she had been attending classes at the university and then she was gone. She knew everyone, including the police, suspected foul play, but with no leads the case went cold.

Blast it, Jane thought. *Why did she have to bring up Jackie?*

"Here's your ticket. Call or text when you get there."

"I will," Jane promised. "Don't worry, mom, I'm going to be on a moving train with lots of people around. I'll be perfectly safe." *Not to mention I'm the fastest girl on the track team. I think can outrun anyone around here.* The platform was mostly empty of people when they arrived, but Jane caught a glimpse of a tall boy her age disappearing into the passenger car.

One of the railroad workers opened the storage compartments on the lower part of the train car to stow the baggage. Jane slipped the latch on her suitcase and locked it shut. She handed the oversized case to the worker and watched as he wrestled it into the right spot in the storage compartment. Her backpack she kept with her as she hugged her mom one last time, and then climbed onto the train and began her freedom of the next four weeks.

"Bye," her mom called.

Jane turned at the top of the stairs and smiled at her mom. There was the hiss of air brakes releasing. Jane waved goodbye, then turned into the passage car. She held on when the first lurch came, then expertly made her way into the car. Slowly the train gathered speed until they were rolling north, hooked to the end of a freight train bound for who knew where.

Jane found a seat on the eastern side of the train so she could watch the countryside and sat down for a while. At first the ride was quiet, as the train gained speed, heading out of the Twin Cities metro area. Soon they were into the country-side, and trees and fields filled the windows on either side of the train. She was just settling in, beginning to enjoy the view, when she heard the scuffle of commotion behind her.

"Hey, watch it!"

Jane turned as the voice shouted from the back of the car. Standing in the middle of the aisle looking towards her was the funny-looking little man with an odd round hat. Lying on the floor at his feet Jane saw a boy almost her own age, maybe a year older.

"I'm sorry," the little man said as he reached down to help the boy up. "I didn't mean to run into you."

"Whatever. Get away from me."

This could be interesting, Jane thought as she pulled her camera out of the backpack at her feet. Carefully she focused between the train seats and snapped a picture of the little man's head as the tall boy stood up under his own power and glared down at him. She looked around but the rest of the passengers had already turned back to their own business, but for some reason Jane found the disagreement amusing, so she kept watching. *Besides* she thought, *the boy is kind of cute.* Then she looked more closely at the little man, and a jolt ran through her. It was the little man from the museum. Suddenly it felt a bit odd that after the chance meeting at the museum that she was seeing the short man again. Still this little man didn't creep her out nearly as much as the guy she had seen in the park. This man might be odd, but in a funny not a crazy insane way.

"Do you like maps?" the little man asked the boy suddenly.

Jane chuckled at the way the little guy's face lit up when he mentioned maps, and she laughed a little louder when she saw the look of confusion fill the boy's face.

"What are you talking about? Maps? No. Get away from me, all right."

Wait a minute. *Maps?* she thought. *What an odd question. Wait a minute,* her mind cried out in alarm. *The strange little man had been asking about maps and compasses in the museum. But was he the same little man I'd seen kicked out of mom's company's lobby?* Suddenly the little man stopped being funny and started being a bit creepy.

She froze as the little man's eyes turned towards her and zeroed in on the small part of her face sticking up above the seat. A moment later the tall boy's eyes looked towards her too, and she ducked below the back of the seat hoping neither of them would come towards her.

"Never mind."

Jane heard the thumps of footsteps on the metal walk between the seats, and she scrambled to get her earphones out of her backpack and plug them into her phone. A moment later a strange face peered at her from the aisle, and the little man cocked his head and stared at her. She hoped he would turn and keep walking. Finally his mouth opened, and he spoke to her. She could see he was speaking, but with the music blaring in her ears, she heard nothing but a low mutter without words.

He rambled on and on, seemingly oblivious to the fact that she had the volume on her earphones crank up as high as it could go to drown him out. Suddenly the battery died in her phone, and she shook her head. *This just isn't my day.* She tapped the edge of the device but was only rewarded with a message telling her that the machine was powering itself off. Then it went blank. Fate was making this conversation happen whether she wanted it or not.

"Do you like maps?" the little man said. "I saw you at the museum looking at the maps. They were very old and contained quite a bit of power even locked away behind the glass. That's a good idea, you know, to keep a collection that old and powerful protected. You never know what might come through them."

Jane pulled the ear buds out and tucked away the phone.

"Do you like maps," the man repeated a bit more forcefully, checking to make sure she was listening.

Don't answer don't answer don't answer she repeated over and over to herself. This time he seemed to have heard her but just continued his dialogue anyway.

"I like maps and compasses." He rambled on without even waiting for an answer. He kept talking to her. Gradually, because Jane really did like maps, she found herself drawn into the description he was giving for maps he had seen and held. It was as though they came alive for him.

"I . . ." Jane started as her naturally polite nature took over. "I think they're kind of interesting." While that wasn't completely true, she was hardly about to tell this little weirdo that she very much enjoyed looking at old maps. Especially those with the little drawings of sea monsters and dragons where people from years ago had been trying to warn others of danger or just trying to make their maps look a bit more interesting.

"Well, good." The little man seemed immensely pleased he had finally drawn her into his conversation. "I love maps . . ."

Oh, no, he's going to sit down, Jane grumbled in her mind. And the empty aisle seat seemed overwhelmingly inviting. Suddenly she picked up her backpack off the floor and plopped it down on the seat next to her. Afraid that the action seemed particularly unfriendly, she began rummaging through the dark interior as she pretended to search for something.

"Do you have any vellum?"

She looked up and groaned on the inside. He was quietly watching her and now waited for her to answer. She couldn't help but notice he wore a pair of trousers that seemed to have been stitched together by hand and his shirt hung almost to knees. His shoes were wooden like those she had seen pictures of in books about people from Scandinavia.

"Huh?" Jane muttered. *What had he asked?*

"Vellum," he repeated. "Vellum's the only thing to draw a real map on. Oh, sure you can use paper and have a pretty drawing. It'll give you directions, maybe help you get across the city, but nothing more. But, when you put a map on vellum or at least leather, ah, then you have something with some power in it."

"But a map is just that, a drawing of places to go. There's no . . . no power in a map," Jane said as she sat up and looked at him.

"Oh, I beg to differ," he said easily. "A well-drawn map can take you many places." he replied. "Even places not of this world."

That's it. Now I know he's completely nuts. Jane looked about for someone to come rescue her but everyone in the compartment seemed to have better things to do at the moment. *Cowards* she thought. *Someone'll come to my rescue and get this little weirdo to leave.*

"Look at this compass," he said, holding something out. "I made it and—" Suddenly he pulled back his hand before Jane had even looked at what he held out, as his attention was drawn away. Then he frowned. "I thought I lost him," he muttered under his breath. "I have to go."

Suddenly there was a commotion at the front of the car. Jane looked up to see a thin man in almost as weird clothing enter the car. He wore a black robe that almost reminded Jane of a priest's robe but this one had a small red mark over the man's heart. His hair was black and greasy, as if it hadn't been washed in days, and she noticed his eyes narrowed when he saw the first little man. In another jolt of déjà vu, Jane realized the black robe with the red emblem was same get up worn by the creep they had spotted at the river. Jane looked around hoping that other people would be watching, but everyone seemed to be engrossed in their own affairs.

"Time to stop running, Tasker," the black-robed man said quietly. "My master has some things he wishes to speak to you about."

"I will never work for Cain," Tasker replied. He looked back at Jane and then over to where the tall boy sat, watching the conversation unfold. He seemed amused by it with the attention directed elsewhere. Tasker turned and walked towards the back of the train as the conductor entered and stepped around the evil-looking man.

"Is there a problem here?" the railroad worker asked.

"No, no problem," hissed the evil-looking man. He shoved past the conductor and walked after Tasker. Moments later he disappeared through the back of the car, and Jane looked over with wide eyes at the boy sitting across from her. He shrugged. Jane leaned back in her seat, shaking her head. What a weird start to her summer. Suddenly she realized that the tall boy had said something and she completely missed it. She looked back at him blankly and with her face turning red.

"What?" Jane asked as she sat up. The first thing she noticed was that he was wearing a varsity football shirt and that his eyes were bluest she had ever seen.

"Hi, my name is Jacob," he repeated slowly. "What's yours?"

"Jane," she replied just as slowly. Suddenly both of them burst out in laughter and the tension drained away.

"Well, that was weird," Jacob muttered as he leaned across the aisle and looked at her with an disbelieving look in his eyes. "That little guy's been following me around for the last hour talking about maps and compasses, and I don't even know what else. I tried to ignore him, but he wouldn't shut up so I finally told him off."

Jane nodded. Jacob was tall with sandy hair that curled back away from his face. He seemed completely at ease as he leaned back comfortably in his seat. Still he kept his eyes riveted on her as he talked.

"So, then I told him, 'Look, I play football, and if you don't get away from me, I'm gonna toss you off this train,'" Jacob said. He paused a moment as he looked at Jane as if to see that she was listening. "I mean that little man was so nuts! He talked to you, too. I bet you thought he was just as crazy." When Jane didn't answer, his face kind of fell. He momentarily looked away, out the window, then turned back. "So where are you headed?" he asked.

Jane shrugged. "Well, there's only one stop for passenger cars on this train. Duluth," Jane replied. Then she thought she had been a little rude by answering so abruptly. *Nice one, Jane. Tick off the really cute guy. Yup, that's the ticket. You'll never get his number that way.*

"Oh, well, yeah," Jacob said as he hung his head.

"No, look I'm sorry," Jane said hastily. "I'm not trying to be rude. I just . . . well, that little guy kind of . . . and then the creepy one . . ."

Jacob's face brightened immediately, and she breathed a sigh of relief. She had been thinking that having a tall, brawny guy as an escort wasn't such a stupid idea. Maybe she could keep him around her until they got off the train and the strangely dressed little men would keep their distance. *You know just to keep me safe,* she rationalized to herself.

"Well, anyway that was really weird. So, are you staying in Duluth long? I live there. Um, I could show you around if you're not so familiar—"

"Ah, crap," Jane burst out suddenly. She looked up just as Jacob's eyes fell again. "No, not you." He brightened again visibly. "Look. That little guy dropped something on the seat here. I really don't want to deal with him again."

"Well, maybe we could see if we can find him and return it," Jacob said as he rose and looked over the edge of her seat at the thing lying there. "What is it?"

"I don't know," Jane said. "It kinda looks like a compass of some sort." Jane replied. She picked up the square box from the seat where it was wedged alongside the cushions. She held it up for him to see, and they both leaned in close to examine it. "Wow," Jane said.

"Yeah, wow," Jacob said. "That's the most intricate, the nicest looking . . . compass I've ever seen."

The compass was square and just filled the palm of Jane's hand. Its edges were engraved with at least a dozen small dials while the top was covered with a large crystal and had a series of what appeared to be movable settings around it. The needle that should have pointed north seemed to be broken, though because the needle swung in lazy circles as they watched. Jane thought, *If it's a compass, it's broken.*

"It doesn't even work," Jacob muttered. "Unless magnetic north is actually circling us."

"That's true, but even broken, this looks like it's valuable. Let me put my stuff in my backpack, and then we can go return it. I don't want anything to do with a crazy person," Jane replied. "And I sure don't want him trying to find me in Duluth." She slipped her camera and earphones back into the pack and then slid her phone into the front pocket of her jeans.

"IPhone?" Jacob asked.

"Yup," Jane responded. "It's the newest one." She patted her pocket and smiled.

"Cool," Jacob responded as he pulled out a similar device from his own pocket. "Version three. I wouldn't mind getting a four, but they're kind of spendy. I have a summer job. I thought it'd give me lots of spending money, but it's only making me enough to keep insurance on my car."

"You got a car?" Jane said suddenly a bit more interested in getting his number. "Oh, I'm so jealous. My mom says I have to wait another year. She let's me drive hers sometimes, but she's so protective of it."

"Well, when we get to Duluth, if you need to go anywhere, I can drive you around," Jacob offered, sounding hopeful.

Jane let the offer hang. Better to keep him wondering, than to agree too readily. Jane hefted the compass in her hand. It was heavy, and she wondered what it was made out of to be so weighty. It almost felt electric, too, like that feeling in the air before a storm that produces a lot of lightening.

"Come on. I'll help you find him," Jacob said with a smile. He stood up and began walking down the center aisle towards the back of the car where the little man had made his exit.

Jane followed him down the aisle, and then stepped into the sheltered area between the cars as he held the door. There was a rush of wind as they entered the second car, and suddenly Jacob stopped ahead of her, and she bumped into him.

"Hey, what are you—" Jane was cut off as Jacob suddenly yelled. He lunged forward, and Jane could see what was going on.

"Get away from him!"

At the end of the car, the greasy looking man in the black robe with the red emblem was leaning over the other little man, who lay on the floor of the car. The greasy man was digging through his pockets. Behind Jane came another shout as the conductor entered the car and saw what was happening.

"Stop!"

The thin man in the black robe turned and fled through the far end of the car. Jacob ran after him, followed by the conductor. Jane was about to follow, but when she reached the collapsed figure, she looked down. He was looking up at her and his hand waved feebly. She skidded to a halt and knelt beside him, cringing at the mass of cuts and bruises that showed on his face. No matter how crazy she thought he was, no one deserved to be beaten up like this.

"Are you all right?" Jane asked as she took a corner of her sweater and dabbed away some of the blood. She shrugged out of her sweater and rolled it into a ball to tuck under his head.

"Did you find it?"

"What?" Jane said. How this little guy could be thinking of anything other than his dire condition was beyond her.

"Did you . . . did you find the compass?" Tasker repeated weakly. He was slipping over the edge of consciousness.

"Well, yes. We were just coming to bring it back to you," Jane said as she tried to press the little box into his hand.

"No," Tasker muttered and shook his head. "You must keep it. One of you must use it. Cain must be stopped." He tried to push her hand and the compass back toward her.

"Who is Cain," Jane said, confused. "I don't know anyone named Cain."

His injured face took on an urgency. "The Adherents are getting ready," Tasker muttered. "You must help us. Above all protect the compass." He pushed the compass back into her hands and folded them around the device. Then he pulled a thick ring from his finger and pressed it into her hand as well. "Take this. Give it to the boy when he returns. Tell no one else what you have. Cain has ears everywhere. There's a roll of vellum in my jacket. Keep it safe along with the pen that's there. They'll be your best friends in time. I made them for you."

Jane was forced to lean close to hear the last of his words. Then he faded into unconsciousness. There was a shout of voices at the back of the car, and Jane shoved the compass into her backpack out of sight. She reached into his jacket pocket and found the roll of what felt like leather. The pen looked odd, old. Nothing like the Sharpies she favored. She leaned back as the little man's eyes fluttered a moment, then slipped shut. She looked about as she slipped the vellum and pen into her pockets on the inside of her wind breaker.

CHAPTER FOUR
Meeting on the Shore

"ARE YOU ALL RIGHT?" Jacob cried when he rushed back into the car followed by the conductor.

"Well yes," Jane answered.

"That guy disappeared," Jacob muttered crossly. He slapped his fist into his hand and shook his head in disbelief.

"How can he get off a moving train?" Jane asked not understanding what they were saying.

"I mean he completely disappeared," Jacob said again. "I mean *poof*, vanished into thin air. We like searched the entire car and there was nothing. He didn't come back through here, did he?"

"No. No, I didn't see him, and he couldn't have gotten past me without my seeing him."

The conductor was kneeling over Tasker, checking his pulse but his face looked worried.

"Will he be all right?" Jacob asked as he joined the older man on the floor of the aisle. He took off his sweatshirt and laid it over the unmoving form in an effort to keep him warm.

"It's hard to tell," the conductor replied. "His pulse is weak, but it seems steady." He retrieved a radio from his belt and spoke into it for a minute then nodded to himself. "We'll have an ambulance standing by in Duluth to pick him up. I'm also sure the police will want to speak to both of you about what happened."

"Why? We didn't do anything," Jane protested vehemently. "We were just trying to help." Suddenly a flashback of the hours she'd spent talking to the police about her parents' whereabouts relating to her sister's disappearance came back to her.

"Young lady, no one said you did anything wrong," the conductor said as he looked at her. "But you're the only ones, besides myself, to get a good look at the man who did this. That makes us all witnesses. The police will want witnesses so when they catch the man who did this they can charge him."

"Oh, right," Jane muttered sheepishly. "Sorry, I'm a little shaken."

A moan drew everyone's attention back to the little man on the floor of the car. Another soft groan escaped from between his lips. The conductor rose and motioned to them. "Stay with him. I need to lock up the car. We're going to be pulling into the Duluth yard in a few minutes. Then the police will take over."

"But what if the other guy comes back?" Jane erupted. The thought of staying at the little man's side with a violent maniac on the loose left her hand shaking and her voice cracking.

"It's all right," the conductor replied. "I'll have Eddy, one of our engineers, come back here to help you keep watch."

At that moment a mountain of a man entered through the back of the car and looked around, his eyes widened slightly as he took in the whole scene, but then they seemed to narrow with determination.

"Eddy," the conductor said, "stay here with these two and keep an eye on the little guy. He's hurt."

"He said his name was Tasker," Jane muttered after the conductor had left the car. "What as odd name. It must be a last name."

"This whole thing's been odd," Jacob agreed. He looked at her and then said. "I suppose we should exchange numbers . . . I mean . . . just in case we need to . . . you know . . . talk about what happened." He finished lamely. Crimson crawled up his cheeks as he shuffled his feet on the rubber padding that covered the passenger car floor.

"Sure thing," Jane murmured as she breathed a sigh of relief. She had been trying to think of a good way to ask for his number without seeming to be too forward or desperate. His asking made her life so much easier even if it cost him some embarrassment. Outside there was a hiss of brakes as the train continued to slow as it neared the train yards of Duluth. They exchanged numbers and saved them into their phones. Jacob even insisted they do a test call to make sure both of them had inputted it correctly.

When the train came to a complete halt, a pair of Duluth city police officers accompanied by an ambulance crew entered the car. Within ten minutes, the little man was whisked away, and Jane hoped he'd be okay. The police officers helped with moving the unconscious Tasker and then returned to question them and the conductor.

Jane and Jacob spent the next twenty minutes telling their story and retelling their story just to make sure both of the officers had the entire thing straight. The officers in turn made notes and then wrote again on those notes as they tried to extract every bit of information they could about the suspected assailant. When Jane and Jacob finally were allowed to exit the train, it was late afternoon. Jane spotted her Grandpa almost immediately. He was standing near the police cruiser, chatting with an officer, but he had a worried look on his face. She waved at him and smiled, then turned back to Jacob.

"Will you walk me over there?" she asked. "My grandpa would love to meet you."

Jacob nodded. He shouldered his own smaller travel bag and then politely picked up her suitcase and motioned for her to lead the way. They crossed over the tracks and walked to where the parking area was cordoned off behind a steel fence.

"Hi, Grandpa," Jane said as she wrapped him in a great big hug.

"Jane, what happened?" Grandpa Arnie asked. "The officer said there'd been trouble on the train." Then looked over and nodded to Jacob with a bit of surprise. "Jake! What are you doing here? I thought you were visiting your dad for the next couple of weeks."

"He conveniently forgot, claimed he was busy, and sent me back," Jacob muttered as he kicked at the dirt. "Mom was so mad she screamed at him until he hung up."

"I bet," Grandpa Arnie replied. "Well, I might as well give you a ride home."

"Wait a minute," Jane said as she looked back and forth between them. "You two know each other?"

"Jacob and his mom own the brown house just down the block from us," Grandpa Arnie explained as he opened the truck on his big Crown Victoria. "Just moved in about eight months ago right?" he glanced over the trunk lid at Jacob.

"Yeah, that sounds about right," Jacob agreed. He picked up Jane's suitcase and his own bag once again and walked to the trunk.

While her big bag had mostly filled her mother's trunk, Granpa's Crown Vic had room for her stuff, Jacob's and room to spare. They put their bags in the trunk. Jane sat down in the front seat, while Jacob slipped into the back seat and slid over to the middle so he could lean forward and talk to them. The story of the strange little man who liked maps and the nasty black-robed man came out in spurts from both of them as Grandpa Arnie threaded his way through downtown Duluth and out past the famous Glensheen Mansion. Finally they pulled off the main road and drove about half way up the hill overlooking Lake Superior. They pulled into the drive of a brown Victorian-style house, and Jacob slid over to the door.

"Thanks for the ride," Jacob said as stepped out of the car.

"Anytime, son," Grandpa Arnie replied as he turned and watched him get out of the back seat. He popped the trunk lever.

Once he had retrieved his bag, Jacob stopped by the passenger window and stood hesitantly for a moment. He seemed to want something else. Finally he leaned over the window and looked at Jane, his face flushed again, "Would you like to go down to the Depot with me sometime, or get something to eat? I have season passes." The words came out in a tumble.

Jane smiled, feeling her own face warm. "I think that would be nice."

Jacob smiled. "Okay I'll call you." He patted his shirt pocket where he had put his IPhone. Then he turned and hurried up the path to the front door, where his mom stood waving to Grandpa Arnie.

Her grandpa beeped his horn in acknowledgment as he put the car in reverse. "He's a nice boy," Grandpa Arnie said as he backed out of the drive and continued down the street to their house. "He mowed the lawn all summer for me while I was taking care of your grandma after her surgery."

Jane nodded. This day had been almost too much for her to keep up with. All she wanted right now as to crawl into bed and get some sleep.

THE NEXT TWO DAYS WERE QUIET as Jane slept late each morning and then spent time talking with her grandma and grandpa.

On Tuesday morning the police came by and spoke with her again. Soon after Jacob showed up at the front door and was let in by her grandpa. His face was troubled as he walked through the short hall leading to the kitchen.

"Did they talk to you too?" Jacob asked. He sat at the dining room table with the three of them drinking a Mountain Dew and trying not to stare at Jane. He fiddled with his phone as if he was waiting for an important call.

"Yes, the officer said the train was completely empty and the little man went missing from the hospital yesterday. They are still trying to figure out how he walked out of a secured room. I don't understand."

"It's weird," Jacob muttered as he took another sip from his can. He seemed to be gathering his courage and finally spoke. "Do you want to go take a walk down by the shore?"

Jane noticed that her grandma and grandpa both hid a smile when Jacob asked, and she frowned at them. "I'd like that, Jacob. Let me grab my windbreaker."

She walked up the stairs to her room and grabbed the light brown jacket from her closet. It seemed heavier than she remembered, and then she remembered she had put the roll of leather and the pen in the inside pocket. On a whim, she grabbed the compass and the ring from the bottom of her backpack and slid them into her pockets as well. This would be the perfect time to take a closer look at what the little man had given her.

"Be careful, Jake . . ." Jane heard her grandpa admonish as she came back down the steps. "They still haven't found the creep who beat up that poor man. And I told you what happened to Jane's sister. That wasn't that long ago, so keep a close eye out for anything out of place."

"It's all right, sir. I'll make sure nothing happens," Jacob replied. "I know most of the people in this town, and if there is anything out of place, I'm sure I'll spot it. We'll be careful, so don't worry."

She came down the stairs just as Jacob walked into the main room of the house and smiled up at her, "Shall we?" Jane grinned back, then gave her grandparents hugs, assuring them she'd be careful, too.

They walked out into the drive and climbed into Jacob's car, which he told her proudly was a 1995 Mustang. The car was midnight blue and had a white racing stripe down the side. When he turned over the engine, it roared to life immediately with a deep, throaty voice. The interior was perfectly clean and waxed until it shown brilliantly, and Jane wondered if she could even sit down without ruining the seats.

Ten minutes later, they were parked at Kitchi Gammi Park and walking along the rock-strewn beach. It was early afternoon and a warm sunny day, so dozens of other people also walked the beach. Jane felt safe. As they walked, they chatted about school and their parents. Jane looked out over the water and noticed idly that two big ore boats moved slowly south, coming closer to the shore. In the bay, a fishing boat lay at anchor. All of them seemed so little compared to the vastness of the lake itself.

"So what do you think happened to . . . what was his name? Tasker?" Jacob asked as they walked towards a heaped up pile of rocks where another couple was sitting. There was plenty of room for private conversations on the tumbled rocks, and they found a spot to sit and enjoy the warm sunshine.

"I don't know. I hope nothing bad happened to him," Jane admitted. "I mean he was strange but he wasn't bad."

They sat there for a while and talked, before moving down the beach again, oblivious to the passage of time and the lowering of the sun in the evening sky.

"Yeah, there are no laws against being strange," Jacob laughed. "If there were, half the world would be in jail."

They walked and talked for another hour before Jane slipped her hands into her pockets and felt the edges of the compass.

"Oh, forgot about this," Jane said. They stopped and sat down on a park bench as she pulled the roll of leather and the ring from her pocket. "Tasker said to give this to you." She handed the ring to Jacob and watched as he turned it over in his hands. It was thick and heavy but surprising it fit his ring finger on his right hand perfectly. Across the surface a gold strip had been inlaid into the darker metal, and it shimmered almost like it was lit from within.

"Wow. I wonder how they managed to get a light inside it. Why do you think he wanted me to have it?" Jacob turned it over in his hands a couple of times. "I don't get it. This has to worth a lot of money. Doesn't it seem odd for a homeless bum to have something like this? I mean who walks around with an expensive ring and an ornate compass dressed in wooden shoes and baggy, hand-stitched pants? Do you still have it . . . the compass I mean?"

"Yeah," Jane pulled the bronze mechanism out of her pocket and they both leaned closer to each other as they looked down at the intricate work. "Look at the sides. I think each of those dials will move. Let's see." She counted as she turned the compass around. Three dials on each side for a total of twelve dials. Each had a series of numbers placed around the edges of the dial. The top held three dials and this time the dials had small images of creatures etched into the top. Some of them were fantastic and looked to be straight out of the *Chronicles of Narnia*. There were twenty-one tiny images on the outermost dial, fourteen on the middle dial and seven on the inner dial. The craftsmanship on the crystal surface made them almost seem alive.

"Why would anyone make such a strange compass?" Jacob said as he carefully turned it over. The bottom was blank except for a small name etched into the bronze—"Tasker." "Look it has the little guy's name etched into the bottom."

The beach had emptied as the sun began to dip lower and lower in the evening sky. From out across Lake Superior a stiff wind arose, and the water filled with white caps. "Shall we get something to eat and find somewhere a bit warmer?"

"Yes, let's," Jane agreed. Suddenly she felt nervous about being out on the deserted beach, and the coming of darkness didn't help what she was feeling. Jacob tucked away the ring, and Jane put the compass back in her pocket. They both rose and began walking back to the parking area when the sound of footsteps behind them drew their attention. They both glanced over their shoulders at the sound. Jane gave an involuntary gasp, and Jacob said, "You! How did you get off the train?"

The black-robed man advanced slowly down the beach toward them. He held a curved dagger and his eyes held death. He raised the knife threateningly and narrowed his eyes as he hissed at them. "Give me the compass."

"No," Jacob growled as they continued to back away from him. He reached into his pocket and passed Jane his keys. Then he pulled his phone from his pocket and dialed 911. He left his finger hovering over the SEND key and waved it at the man. "Get away from us or I'm calling the police."

"The what?"

"The police. You know the guys with the big guns."

The robed man seemed confused by the phone and its shining screen because his eyes were drawn to it as the signal connected. Suddenly there was a brilliant flash of light, and a moment later the small form of Tasker appeared on the beach.

"You better run, Adherent," Tasker threatened. "I don't have to hide what I can do here where no one is watching."

"What about them, little man." the Adherent muttered, indicating Jane and Jacob. "What of your precious Divide, you start using your magic here, and you know what will happen to the Divide."

"Maybe over time," Tasker replied. "But that will hardly help you."

The Adherent's eyes narrowed as he fingered his knife. For a moment Jane thought he was going to attack them anyway. Then he suddenly turned and slipped into the darkness and was gone.

CHAPTER FIVE
In This World

WOW! THANKS! I THOUGHT HE was going to try to kill us," Jacob said as he turned off his phone. He reached to Tasker to shake his hand, but the little man batted it away.

"I told you to protect the compass not pull it out where every Adherent in the area can feel its presence and report to Master Cain where it is," Tasker growled. "Put it back in your pocket at the very least."

"Whoa," Jane said as her brow furrowed down. "You haven't told us anything, least of all why some creep would be willing to kill for a little bronze box of a compass that doesn't even work."

"It most certainly *does* work," Tasker said indignantly. He puffed out his chest and glared at her. "Why would you think it doesn't?"

"I have never seen a compass that seems to point in random directions," Jane said as she pulled it out of her pocket and pointed to the crystal. "Compasses are supposed to point towards magnetic north. Yours doesn't."

He gave her a disgusted look. "Compasses are supposed to bring one to their destination. Who says your destination is always north of you? That would be an idiotic condition to build into a compass." Tasker stepped up to Jane, reached out and closed her fingers around the compass and pushed back at her with a shove. "Now put that away before more Adherents gather and they decide to test my resolve."

"Let's get off the beach," Jacob said suddenly. "Where did you come from just now?"

Tasker cocked his head and pointed. "I was just over there. Why?"

"No . . . no. There was a loud flash and crack, and then you were just there, like you appeared from nothing."

Tasker smiled. "You want to stick to that story, boy? I just appeared out of nothing?"

Jacob turned a number of shades of red. After casting Jane a glance, he shrugged. "I'm hungry. Jane and I were just going to get some food."

Jane nodded, then shivered as another blast of cool air swept off Lake Superior. With the sun now setting beyond the expanse of the city it was getting colder, though she felt it had nothing to do with the weather.

As they hurried back to the Mustang, Tasker stayed with them. When Tasker struggled with the door handle, it was clear he meant to come with them. Jane met Jacob's eyes, then moved up beside him and helped. "It works like this."

"Ahh," Tasker muttered. "I thought it was something like that, but I wasn't sure."

"How can you not know how to open a door handle?" Jacob said with a chuckle as they climbed in. He turned the engine over. When it roared to life, Tasker jumped at the sound. Jacob looked in the rearview mirror as he slipped the car into gear.

"Where I come from we don't have much use for 'cars' as you call them," Tasker muttered and he leaned back.

"Put your seatbelt on," Jacob muttered.

"What?"

"Oh, my goodness! They don't have seat belts where you live either?" Jacob said with a raised eyebrow. "Look it's the law, and I'm not paying a ticket because you can't figure out how to clip the belt together. It's hard enough to get a full tank of gas and insurance out of my paychecks."

"Just drive," Jane said. "I want to get out of here." There was a flash in the shadows as Jacob flipped on the headlights, and she could have sworn she saw that Adherent character running across the parking area towards them. "Go!" she cried out. She reached over her shoulder and hit the lock on her door, her heart racing as she searched the darkness until she spotted the shadowy character.

Jacob might have missed the arrival of the first robed figure, but not the second and a third. Robed figures seemed to be erupting from the darkness. "Hold on!" he shouted and slammed the car into reverse. He gunned the engine, spraying rocks and dust across the approaching shadows. The Mustang's front end whipped around, and he expertly flipped the machine back into drive and tapped the gas just enough to keep the spray of rocks flying and to send the vehicle roaring out of the parking area. He hit London Road with a squeal of tires as the vulcanized rubber caught. The parking lot vanished as they raced away.

"That was close," Tasker muttered as he slid back across the leather seat and rubbed the side of his head where it had bumped against the window. "Try not to pull out the compass until we are ready to use it. You have to learn to shield its location a bit better. Even taking it out of your pocket in the open like that is like drawing flies to honey."

"Sorry," Jane muttered. "You haven't explained any of this."

"Do you have the map I gave you?" Tasker asked.

Jane looked out driver's window across from her and caught a glimpse of Lake Superior through the trees. The moon was brilliant, and it lit the lake with brilliance. Across the surface of the water a huge wave rolled and seemed to be chasing them. It gathered the two cargo ships and hauled them along to ride like surf boards atop the crest of the water.

"Jacob, we need to higher ground," Jane said quietly.

"What?" Jacob looked at her not understanding.

"Higher ground. NOW!" Jane shouted as she pointed out the window. The wave was about a half mile from the shore and closing fast, the bobbing lights of one of the cargo vessels shown weakly from the top of a fifty-foot wall of water.

Jacob shouted something that came out garbled and then pulled the wheel to the right and pushed the gas pedal to the floor. The needle on the speedometer passed fifty within mere moments. Thankfully the road climbed steeply as they rocketed inland away from the wave.

Jane craned her head around and thought she saw the leering face of the Adherent staring down at them from high atop the wave. Then the sight was lost from view as Jacob turned down another side street and raced towards her grandpa's house.

The wave wasted its strength against the rocks and buildings closest to the ocean. Behind them was the sickening crunch of wooden homes as the water brought its horrible force to bear on the homes and popular businesses that lined the streets closest to the lake front. Then the water swept back out into the icy depths of the lake, leaving instant destruction in its wake. Car alarms pierced the night and the shouts of survivors filled the air as people emerged from the devastated buildings. The great bodies of the cargo ships lay broken and battered across the neighborhoods closest to the lake.

"That was close," Tasker muttered. "Too close." He craned his head around to look out the rear window of the Mustang.

"Close, whatever or whoever did that just destroyed dozens of houses," Jacob erupted. "I'd say they succeeded in whatever they were trying to do."

"No, they didn't, and you made them waste a good bit of their power in that failure. It'll take Cain some time to build up that kind of strength to use in this world," Tasker said and he almost sounded happy. "It takes a lot of strength to push something like that through the Divide. Besides, I believe he was trying for the two of you."

Jacob slared at him. "What did you say?"

"He wasted his power trying to get us and failed." Tasker rubbed a growing bruise on his head.

"No after that?" Jane asked. "What came after he had wasted his power?"

"In this world?" Tasker asked.

"Yes, that bit," Jane turned and looked at him. "What do you mean exactly by 'in this world'? Where do *you* live?"

"I live right here," Tasker said. He pointed up the hill to where the well-lit Enger Tower pierced the sky. "My cottage is just north of Lookout Tower."

"You mean Enger Tower," Jacob corrected him. "I've lived in this city my whole life, and it's always been called Enger Tower."

"In my world it's called Lookout Tower. Now it serves as a watch post for the Adherents." Tasker leaned back and rubbed his eyes. "We should get inside somewhere. They'll have a harder time tracking us if we're inside. Walls and ceilings muffle the signature of the compass, drawing its power."

"My mom's working. We can go to my place," Jacob said. He slipped the Mustang back into gear and started working his way through the side streets clogged by curious onlookers and people rushing to help with the devastation below them. Fifteen minutes later the Mustang was parked in Jacob's garage, and they were sitting in his basement listening to the roar of the police and fire sirens responding to the path of destruction carved by the wave.

"Now please explain some of this to us so that we can understand it," Jane said tiredly. Her whole body felt exhausted as though she had just run a race as fast as she could.

"First show me the compass. I'll help you learn to shield it."

Jane pulled the bronze box from her pocket and held it out to Tasker. He took it and gave the dials at the top an expert twist, adjusted several of the side dials and handed it back.

"Adjust the dials every day. That tunes the compass to a different frequency each day and makes it harder for them to track the signal."

"Can't we just take the batteries out and shut down the signal?" Jacob asked. He threw his body down in the corner of the couch and rubbed his face. Jane could see he was stressed.

"Where do you put the batteries?" Jane said. Suddenly she pulled out her phone. "Wait. I haven't texted my mom today. I don't want her to worry." *Mom I am good just got back from a nice walk on the beach.*

She immediately got back, *OK J. stay safe.*

When Tasker had her attention again, he said, "There are no batteries. The compass draws its power directly from the magnetic fields around the earth. I assumed people here understand how to tap into that."

"Um, no, we use batteries," Jane said.

Tasker sighed. "Look, have you ever wondered where some legends come from? Why ancient peoples had pictures of . . . sea monsters and dragons on their maps? Where did the creatures of legend in mythology come from? Where did many of the great writers of your time come up with their ideas?"

"Overactive imaginations?" Jacob quipped as he popped open a can of pop and took a gulp. "Anyone else want something to drink? I have Mountain Dew, Cherry Pepsi, Root Beer, and a few other kinds in here." He took another gulp and coughed as some Mountain Dew slipped down the wrong way and nearly made him spray the liquid from his nose. He pointed to the refrigerator against the wall behind him.

"I'm good," Jane replied.

"Look, these unexplained images come from my world," Tasker said. "Long ago our two worlds existed side by side. Mortals who possessed certain skills—on both sides—were able to cross over at will. Then almost five thousand years ago a council convened. It was decided that the two worlds would be better served being separated, so the Divide was put in place. The two worlds continue to live next to each other but never again would they meet. Indeed if the worlds come together now, there'll be untold misery. You see, my world is a world of magic and fairy tales, where creatures from the imaginations of people really do exist. Your world is a world of science and structure where there is no longer a place for magic."

"So who is this Cain fellow?" Jane asked suddenly.

"He's a powerful ruler in my world. He's used his control over a group called the Adherents to conquer and enslave much of the lands around here," Tasker said. "He's begun finding ways to fuse magic and technology. He likes technology. He seeks a way to enter this world, which is rich in that way, so he may increase his technology and conquer both worlds."

"Looks like he already found a way to send his Adherents to our world," Jacob muttered. He finished the pop and tossed the can into a nearby trash container.

"Oh, he's managed to get a few through but at horrible cost," Tasker muttered. "The Divide still holds strong in most places, but he's trying to weaken it. You see there is one way to move between the worlds, there are maps laid down in ancient times by which a certain special few may move freely from world to world without harming the Divide. They were created because a few of the ancients believed that someday the worlds could come back together. Someday when the human race was more accepting of those things that looked and seemed strange. While I don't believe that's possible they believed it. So a way was made."

Jane and Jacob looked at each other. Jacob crossed his eyes for a moment and rolled his head around.

"I am not crazy!" Tasker shouted suddenly at him. "This is serious, I came here seeking what we call a cartographer in my world, that special someone who can use the ancient maps to do more than just move freely between the worlds. This is the only way to stop Cain and his plans for conquest. You think that wave he just raised was bad?" Tasker pointed toward where police and fire trucks were racing to the devastated part of town. "He can kidnap people from this world and send them through the Divide, but they can only pass through once. To try again would kill them without the proper preparations and an anchor. He can create thin places in the Divide to reach through with his power and stir up the waters and do things that people here will think odd but won't raise too much suspicion. He also has been seeking a cartographer with the power to bring the old magic of the maps back to life. Oh, he knows how to send people through the Divide and he can send his power through the maps to create waves and shake the earth but he lacks the true power of a cartographer."

Something jogged into place for Jane. He had first spoken to her at the museum at the map exhibit. "You think it's me," she said, shaking her head. "If I'm what you call a map maker or cartographer, why would I cross over?" Jane asked, her mind racing. "No, that doesn't make sense. Wouldn't that be playing right into his hands?"

"It's what he wants, to bring you to our world where he can capture you, yes. But it's also the only way to stop him," Tasker hurried on. "Besides he already stole something that was very dear to you. You see, I believe he found out about you before I did, found out that you had been born. I think he's been tracking you for some time. In fact, I believe he used his power to kidnap your sister—"

"What!" Jane was on her feet instantly. "What?"

Tasker pressed his palms down in a calming motion. "He thought she was the cartographer. When he realized she wasn't he thought he'd made a mistake. It's taken him since her kidnapping to rebuild his power to pierce the Divide again."

Jane sat back onto the couch. *No it wasn't possible.* "The police said that she was probably kidnapped by someone from out of the area."

"They had that much right," said Tasker.

Jane felt cold inside. A shiver broke through her body as a cold sweat covered her brow at the same time. "Is she alive?" she murmured. An image of her sister's face flashed in her mind—dark hair with crimson highlights, a ready smile and laugh for anyone, deep-blue eyes like her own. Stunned, she collapsed to the couch then snapped to her feet again. "IS SHE ALIVE!" she screamed.

"I believe so," Tasker replied in the low tone. "But I do not know for sure. I caught glimpses of someone almost a year ago. All I saw was blue eyes and a beautiful smile. I believed it was a vision of you. I didn't realize what Cain was doing until I felt the Divide sunder for a moment."

"Why didn't you protect her?" Jane said suddenly. She glared down at the little man. "If you saw her, you should have called the police. You should have protected her!" she shouted. In a moment the fury left her and tears welled up in her eyes as she thought about her sister alone in a strange world and imprisoned by strangers. All the feelings that had haunted her for months after Jackie's disappearance returned full force. She slumped back into the couch again as sobs shook her.

"Nice job, shorty," Jacob growled as he crossed to the couch and put his arms around Jane comfortingly. Jane clung to him as she sobbed.

"I tried," Tasker pleaded desperately. "In this world, I am only one small dwarf. What was I supposed to do against Cain and his Adherents? I have a small bit of power yet, but not enough to stop all of them, not here. In my world I might stop a few of them but not Cain, not anymore. I gave up that strength."

"Just go away and leave me alone," Jane sobbed.

"But—" Tasker started. A glance from Jacob cut him off.

"I think you better go," Jacob said.

"I will go, but please remember to change the dials each day," Tasker pleaded as he gently laid the compass on the coffee table. "If you change your mind, align the crystals on the top of the compass and I will find you if I'm able."

"Just go," Jane sobbed again as she clung to Jacob and fought against the next wave of tears.

Tasker nodded and walked to the glass door to the patio. Then he stopped and looked back at them with a mist of tears in his eyes. He had been so close to finding the one who had the power to save his world and now he was leaving empty handed.

Jacob blinked. One moment the short figure stood by the door. The next he was simply gone. The glass sliding door had not been opened, but the figure of Tasker was no longer in the room. It was as if he had never been there at all.

"I need to get home and check on Grandma and Grandpa," Jane said suddenly. She let go of Jacob as if realizing she was in Jacob's arms for the first time. Hesitantly she rose and gathered up the compass from the table. She turned to Jacob and smiled, "Thanks."

"Anytime," Jacob smiled. "It wasn't exactly the way I had our date planned, but it certainly was exciting—"

"Why don't you call me tomorrow," Jane blurted out. She blushed, lowered her voice and said, "We need to talk about this some more." Jane edged towards the stairs. "Right now I simply want to get to familiar surroundings," she said *and deal with the storm of emotions swirling around inside my head.*

"Sounds perfect," Jacob replied as he followed her up the steps, and then slipped around her to open the front door. "Do you want me to walk you back?" He leaned on the door and looked down at her concern-filled his eyes.

"No . . . if the little man is to be believed," she said, "and I really don't know what to believe, the . . . Adherents have used up enough . . . power that I should be safe for a while. I need some time to think," Jane said as she stepped out the door.

For a moment they both listened to the cacophony of noise the wave's destruction had called. From the swirling lights they could see, it seemed the damage was limited to the riverside area. The city rose so steeply from the lake that just a few streets away from the shore could not have been touched.

"I hope no one died," Jane said.

"We'll find out in the news tomorrow I expect," Jacob said. He put an arm around her shoulders.

Jane looked up at him and smiled through her tears. "I actually had some fun tonight, but you still owe me a meal and some ice cream." She leaned against him uncertain if he would understand her attempt at a joke but hoping he would.

"How about tomorrow night?" Jacob asked. He grinned at her widely, and leaned down towards her. Their lips met once, and then she was gone down the front walk and galloping along the street towards her grandparents' home. He watched her until she disappeared safely through her grandparents' front door and then closed his door slowly. He heard a car pull in, and a few minutes later his mom walked in the side door from the garage.

N
W ← 55 → E
S

CHAPTER SIX
The Master Wants You

JANE AWOKE THE NEXT MORNING with a start, for a moment unsure where she was. She heard dishes clinking downstairs and got a whiff of oatmeal cooking. Suddenly the events of the night before flooded back to her. She remembered walking into the house and hugging her grandparents as relief flooded their faces. She told them of the race uphill in front of the wave but left out the more fantastic parts of the tale. Then she sent a quick text to her mom to let her know she was still fine and went to bed.

Jane rose, showered, fixed her hair. Her mom texted her as she was resetting the dials on the compass.

Were u near the wave?

Jane winced. *No. long ways away*, she lied. She couldn't have her mother trying to come get her, not now, not before she could decide what she needed to do. She closed the text screen and went downstairs.

"Jane," Grandpa Able said when he saw her coming down the steps.

"Hi, Grandpa," Jane replied as she slid into a chair at the small table sitting in the kitchen. Her grandparents' house was a quaint little Cape Cod style with most of the rooms on the main floor except for a guest bedroom and bathroom on the second story.

"Are you all right?" Grandpa Able asked. "I saw on the news this morning what happened last night. I can't believe another wave hit the shore."

Jane impulsively jumped up to give him a tight hug. It meant so much to her that his first thought was to check on her safety. She clung to him as she fought back the tears and then finally returned to her chair when her emotions were back in check.

"What a mess from last night," Grandpa Able muttered as he fumbled with the remote of a small TV mounted to the ceiling and lowered the volume. "The whole town is full of reporters covering this last disaster. They are calling them rogue waves says it happens in the ocean all the time they just don't normally see it happen on a lake very often."

"Was anyone hurt?" Jane asked quietly. Her greatest fear at the moment was being sent home before she made up her mind what she had to do. She had to minimize her involvement of the night's drama. Before her grandfather could answer her question, they heard the tap-slide of the walker. "Grandma!" Jane smiled happily as her white haired grandmother entered the kitchen slowly pushing her walker in front of her.

"Jany," Grandma Kay replied with a smile. "I don't move as fast as I used to with this new knee but I still get around." They both laughed as she sat down at the table.

She wrapped her grandma in a huge hug before returning to her place at the table and dipping her spoon into the bowl oatmeal. She smiled as she ate the brown-sugar-covered oatmeal. What would her friends say if they saw her eating oatmeal and actually enjoying it? That was what she loved about the summer trips to Duluth and staying with her grandparents. There was no pressure to be something she was not or act how her friends thought she should. With her grandparents she could be exactly how she was.

"What are you planning today?" Grandpa Able asked quietly when he finally sat down at the table with his own bowl of steaming hot oatmeal. The spoonful of brown sugar he sprinkled over the top of it melted quickly. Soon he had small rivers of liquid sugar pooling in the dips of the oatmeal. Just how he liked it.

"Well, Jacob wanted to buy me some ice cream, but that wave came in. I was hoping we could go for a walk up around Enger tower, if you didn't mind," Jane said with a smile. "But first, Grandma and I are going to play a round of Scrabble—that is if she has time."

Grandma Kay smiled and nodded. "I always have time for a game of Scrabble."

They finished their late breakfast and cleaned up. By the time the Scrabble game was done—won by Grandma Kay as usual— it was nearly one in the afternoon. After a quick lunch, Jane sent a text to Jacob. She told him about the planned walk at Enger Park with her grandpa. She said she'd stop by his house afterwards.

The drive to Enger Park was uneventful. Jane found herself amazed that so much of the city seemed immune to the chaos on the northern lake shore. But when they arrived at the parking area, Jane was surprised to find it packed with cars and, even worse, packed with vans all with news logos printed on the side. The park around Enger Tower was crowded, and a line of people with cameras anxiously waiting for a chance to get to the top of the structure to snap a photo of the carnage below.

"Vultures," Grandpa Able muttered as they walked by the crowded line and started down one of the paths. "So anxious to record the misery of others that they can't even take time to go help. If I were ten years younger, I would be down there digging through the rubble."

There were two more news crews out in the middle of a wide grassy area of the park interviewing people, and Jane steered her grandpa away from the big cameras. She wanted nothing to do with the news reporters. She'd had her fill of them when her sister disappeared.

"It's all right, girl," Grandpa Able said as he patted her arm. "I won't let them talk to you."

"Thanks," Jane smiled at her grandpa and wrapped her arm a little tighter around his arm. They threaded their way away from that area and circled around the gardens and the path that would lead them closer to the overlook. Here they paused for a little while before finally making their way back to the parking area.

"Look there she is!"

Jane was caught off guard when a reporter stepped out from behind a plain white van followed by a recording crew and turned a microphone towards her.

"Jane Timbrill how are you today? I covered the disappearance of your sister, Jackie Timbrill, almost a year ago. Can you tell us if there have been any updates regarding her assumed kidnapper and what of your father? Have you spoken to him recently?"

The microphone was pointed at her, and the reporter looked at her expectantly. "I . . ."

"Now see here," Grandpa Able started in as he pushed the microphone away. "Have you no respect for the grief my family has already suffered? All that's happening around this city right now, and you choose to drag my family through the mud again!" He opened the car door and hurried Jane into the passenger's seat. "Go destroy someone else's life you, filthy animal."

The reporter smirked as he motioned for the film crew to keep the tape rolling, "You heard the words here first, folks. There might be interesting things happening in the Timbrill kidnapping again. What else would explain such anger? Why else would they be so . . ."

The rest of the words were lost as Jane pulled the door shut and stared straight ahead in horror. A moment later her grandpa got into the car and started the engine. "I'm so sorry, Jany," he said.

"It's not your fault, Grandpa," Jane said as tears started down her face. "Let's just go home."

He nodded and put the car into gear, they pulled out of the parking lot slowly. Suddenly Grandpa Able slammed on the breaks. "Get outa of the road you weirdo," he shouted, waving his hand. "I mean what kind of idiot walks around in a black robe on a hot day?"

Jane lifted her head, horrified to see the black-robed man from the day before staring at her as they drove out of the parking area. They quickly left him behind and turned onto Piedmont Avenue, heading back to I-35, the quickest route to East Superior Street and the fastest way home.

"He looked like he was looking right at us," Grandpa Able muttered. "This town gets stranger every year. If your grandma wasn't in such poor health I'd move back to Grand Marias and get away from this city."

Jane sat slumped in the seat. She just wanted to go back to her room at her grandparents' house and crawl under the covers. What if she went out with Jacob, and the reporter found her again? She wasn't sure she could handle something like that happening again. What if the black-robed man came?

It was almost four in the afternoon when they got home, and Jane fled to her room the moment she walked in the door. Her phone chirped twice telling her there was a text message waiting for her, but she couldn't answer it. She just wanted to be alone. She slipped into her bed and pulled the covers up around her as the tears for her sister started once more, then she drifted off to sleep. The phone messages went unanswered.

JANE AWOKE WITH A START and looked around. All was silent in the house, and it was dark outside her window. She lay in bed trying to shake off the confused stupor of sleep when the sound that woke her came again. A small scratching sound, almost like something or someone was trying to pry a window open. Suddenly her thoughts turned to the compass and she reached under her pillow where the bronze compass was stashed. She held it up and turned one of the small dials on the side over a notch. *Was that enough or do I need to change them all?* The scratching sound became a bit rougher, and she thought it was coming from just outside her window. She changed two more of the dials and then tucked the compass into her pocket. Ever so slowly she rolled over in her bed and looked at the small window. She nearly screamed when a pale face appeared behind the glass for a moment and then disappeared again. Quickly she rolled out of her bed and fluffed her pillow up under the covers, and then she scrambled into the closet before the face appeared once again.

"Thank you, Grandpa," Jane whispered as she put her hand down and it closed around the aluminum softball bat that her grandparents had bought for her nearly five years ago. Suddenly the scratching at the window stopped, and she heard the window being pushed up. There was a rustle of cloth as someone climbed through the window. She raised the bat carefully and watched as a dark figure approached her bed, quietly she eased the closet door open and stepped out behind him and raised the bat. Putting all of her might behind the swing, she brought down the bat. It caught the figure in the middle of the back and dropped him across the bed. There was a groan as she raised the bat again and a flash of black robes as the figure tried to avoid the descending blow. The bat clunked loudly off his skull, and the pale eyes rolled back in his head.

Jane reached over and flipped the light on and looked down, the face of the reporter from earlier in day looked back up at her. This time the man was dressed in black robes, and the small red symbol was emblazoned over his chest. She leaned closer and looked at the symbol. It looked like a sea monster, the kind she had seen drawn on old maps. She wondered exactly what it was supposed to mean. The symbol was made of metal and appeared to be pinned to the robes. She gritted her teeth and stepped close enough to the inert body that she could fumble with the latch. In a minute her finger found how to unfasten the metal clip holding it in place. It was surprisingly tough, and she smiled triumphantly when she finally managed to remove it. The moment she removed it, she stumbled backwards as the figure began to stir. She leapt back, dropping the small medallion. She grabbed her bat again.

"What have you done?" the figure said in a raspy, almost hissing voice, his hands frantically patting the front of his robe. "Where is my anchor?"

"What?" Jane replied. She raised her bat threateningly. "What anchor? What are you talking about? Why are you here?"

"The master wants you."

Jane stumbled back as the figure seemed to begin to dissipate into the air. It was a slow process. The edges of his body began almost to come apart and fade into nothing. It seemed to cause him no pain, his body just lost its solid look and began to fade. He looked up at her with a look of pure horror and reached toward her, his hands like claws.

"Killing me will not stop the others from finding you." The pale face muttered. Suddenly the black-robed figure's body flared with light. A moment later nothing remained of the black-robed man, as though it had never been there in the first place.

Jane was stunned—a person had just vanished before her. Right before her own eyes someone had vanished, not died or anything like in the movies but vanished into thin air. There was another sound from the edge of the bed, and she raised her bat to strike. But then she saw it was her phone flashing and vibrating. She grabbed it and flipped through the texts. It was nine at night, and she had three messages from Jacob and one from her mom. She flipped open Jacob's first and typed out a quick apology.

Sorry about tonight. U wake?

Her phone flashed a minute later, as Jacob's answer filled the screen, *Yes, its ok.*

Can you come over?

Sure? Will your grandpa mind?

No.

BRT

She sent a quick text to her mom saying that she was fine and then tossed down her phone and looked at the now empty bed, she held up the bat limply in her hands as she sat down in a small chair pulled up before her mom's old writing desk. Suddenly she heard a light knock at the front door, and her phone chirped at her again.

I am here.

k

She hurried down the stairs and crossed to the front door. Jacob stood nervously on the front porch looking around. She undid the locks and opened the door for him.

"What happened? I thought we were going to go get ice cream?" Jacob asked in a hurt tone. Then he saw the frightened look on her face and his voice ground to a halt.

"Something came up," Jane replied. "And then I fell asleep without my alarm set. Mostly though it was the creep who just broke into my room and tried to kill me."

"Whoa! What happened?" Jacob said entirely too loudly. He looked around, searching the dark shadows of the house for signs of danger.

She motioned for him to be quiet, and they crept up the stairs to her room. Once inside and the door was closed, Jane slumped down on the edge of the bed and shook her head. "Someone broke in through my window. He was dressed in a black robe like that creep on the beach. What did Tasker call them—Adherents?"

"What happened to him?" Jacob asked as he examined the window. He poked his head out the open window and looked down at the sill and then at the sides. There were a number of gouges in the wood like someone had been trying to claw through the sill. He didn't mention to her that the marks could not have come from a human hand. They truly were claw marks.

"I hit him on the head with my bat," Jane muttered. She rolled the instrument around in her hand once and suddenly realized that a bit of hair still clung to the spot where she had struck the Adherent. "Ick!" Jane yelped and dropped the bat on the floor of her room. It clunked to the ground with a solid thump and she cringed again as the sound echoed through the house.

"What?" Jacob asked as he turned back from the window. He pulled it shut again, and flipped the latches so that it was locked from the inside.

"His hair is still stuck to the bat." She shuddered as she pointed at the grim reminder of what had happened.

Jacob chuckled, "Cool, I have never gotten to tag anyone with a bat that hard."

"Well, next time I'll ask the guy to wait so *you* can hit him," Jane muttered crossly. "It did feel good, though, to smack him on the head that hard."

"Well, what happened to him?" Jacob asked as he sat down in the chair across from her. He picked up the back and flipped it around to examine the bit of hair still clinging to the aluminum. It looked bristly, almost like the rough hair of cows or horses from what he could see, but there was nothing they could gain from it unless they went to the police. He doubted Jane wanted that kind of attention.

"Remember that little red pin that the creep down at the beach was wearing?" Jane said suddenly. She leaned over and searched around on the floor until she spotted the pin under her bed. "Blast it. I can't reach it. Grab that, would you?" she pointed to where it had ended up underneath her bed.

"Sure," Jacob leaned over and looked down to where she was pointing. He could see the pin lying there with the sharp needle sticking out at an angle. To reach it, he was forced to lie down on the floor and reach his arm as far under the bed as he could. He felt around carefully, not wanting to stab his finger, but he still jumped when he managed to prick the tip of his finger with the needle.

"Ouch! Dang thing is sharp," Jacob muttered.

"Don't jab it into your finger. Just pick it up," Jane said as she leaned over and looked under the bed.

Jacob wrapped his hand around the emblem and closed his fingers carefully this time, avoiding the sharp point of the needle and putting his thumb on the flat surface. He stood up and grinned triumphantly. "I got it." He turned it slowly in his hands, staring at it.

Suddenly he looked around and cocked his head to the side. The room was spinning slightly around him. He stumbled back until he ended up sitting on the bed. "What's happening?"

All around him the room began to fade, becoming almost insubstantial. He could see Jane reaching to him, and he reached to her. But he couldn't touch her. Then, with a flash of light, she was gone and so was the room around him. Then he was falling into darkness and the world went black.

CHAPTER SEVEN
The Black Wing Awaits

J ACOB AWOKE WITH A START when something wet touched his face. At first he smiled as it tickled his cheek, but then he felt slobber on his neck. Suddenly his eyes shot open, and he looked up into the face of a mangy-looking black dog. He blinked rapidly to try to clear the watery tears that filled them and looked around. The dog seemed to think he wanted to play. The mutt wagged his tail happily and crouched down with a playful shake. Jacob pushed the creature away and tried to place his surroundings.

He appeared to be lying in a dirty alley between two stone-walled buildings. The ground under him was hard-packed dirt, and he didn't recognize any of the buildings. He could tell he was lying on a slope. As his balance returned, he raised his head carefully and looked out over the steep hill and out across a vast lake that look exactly like Lake Superior. Above him the sky was blue, but there were so many plumes of smoke that it almost seemed like a storm approached on the horizon.

"Uhh, where am I," Jacob muttered. He stumbled to his feet and pushed the mangy dog away from him again. The dog cocked his head to the side and examined him for a moment. He must have decided that this human was not worth his time, because he whined once before turning and trotting off between the buildings in search of more promising amusement. Jacob felt like he had been struck by a freight train or tackled by a football line man. His body hurt, but the pain began fading as he stood and moved his arms and legs about. In a few minutes, he was feeling almost normal.

Jacob leaned heavily on the stone wall to his right and finally made his way to where the alley seemed to connect to a larger road. There was a steady stream of people all dressed in dirty clothes and covered with mud on the wide dirt trail before him. Accompanying this crowd were almost a dozen men on horses and carrying whips.

"What in the world?" Jacob muttered. When he leaned his hand on the wall, he realized he was still carrying the medallion in his hand, and he quickly closed the clasp and slipped it into his pocket. Suddenly he heard a shout and a clatter of hooves. Jacob looked up into the sharp end of a sword held by one of the riders. Two others held old-style muskets with flared barrels on him.

"What are you doing here?" one of the men shouted at him. "This street was ordered cleared for prisoner transport. You will be placed under arrest unless you can show the proper identification."

Jacob shook his head and shrugged. "I don't have any."

"Take him into custody and put him in chains. Another slave for the mines."

The two men on either side of the speaker leapt off there mounts and grabbed Jacob from either side. The men were all wearing black trousers and rough leather boots. The officer was also dressed in a leather vest that was painted black and pinned with a pair of bars that looked suspiciously like fingers to Jacob's sodden mind. His arms were twisted behind him and held firm. The ruffians on either side of him begin to check his pockets.

When they reached the medallion, suddenly the men let go of him and stumbled back.

"What are you doing, fools?" the officer shouted. "Clap him in irons."

"But sir, he's carrying an anchor. He's one of them. You know the crossing affects them sometimes."

The officer's face went pale and he nearly fell from his mount in his hurry to reach the ground. He knelt before Jacob. "I'm sorry, sir. We thought you was one of the rebels tryin to escape."

Jacob pulled himself together as quickly as he could. He managed to wave his hand in what he hoped was an imperious way, "Quite all right. I'm just a little groggy is all."

"Did you just get back from . . . well, 'you know where'? Is it like what they say?" the officer stood, looking nervous and awkward as his men crowded closer. "Rumor is the humans on that side are all soft and rich. Master Cain says when we take control of their side of the Divide, we will all own a dozen slaves and never have to work again." There was a dreamy look in the officer's eyes as he talked.

Jacob's mind had finally cleared enough to begin to follow what was going on. He nodded quickly, "Oh, yes, soft, easy pickings to anyone with half a brain." He smiled and winked. "And we have at least that much, don't we, lads?"

There was a round of half cheers as several of the dirtier men tried to follow him and then just gave up and smiled widely.

"I suppose you'll be wanting to report in so we better move on," the officer said with a half bow. "If you need a ride to Madeline Island, our ship is leaving tonight. I'm sure the captain would be honored to have one so high in the hierarchy of the Adherents aboard." The officers eyebrows raised slightly as he offered the ride.

"Yes, I will look into my last few . . . items that I need to . . . well take care of and then see what happens," Jacob finished awkwardly.

The officer smiled broadly as he took Jacob's words as a yes and vaulted back onto his mount.

"Our ship is the *Black Wing*. It's docked in pier seven," he said with a smile. "I will tell the captain to expect you tonight."

Jacob nodded his agreement and stayed watching as the mounted men gathered up the chained figures and started them down the hill once again. The officer stayed near him. Then his eyes widened even more. The prisoners they escorted were small, short versions of men. They bore an uncanny resemblance to Tasker. Halfway back the row was a pair of tall women with pointed ears, while stumbling at the back of the line, under the weight of a heavy chains was the likeness of huge man with the head of a bull.

"Bah! They call these rebels," the officer said with a sneer. "We caught them running for the western wilds near the border. They were more interested in running then fighting. Still we lined up a few and had the boys shoot them just to make sure the rest remember who runs this territory."

Jacob nodded as he watched the beaten figures trudge down the hill. There were nearly fifty in all, and only half of them were what he would term human. He almost thought he was watching the pictures of one of the books he enjoyed as a little boy come to life.

"Want to kill one for the fun of it?" the officer asked him suddenly.

Jacob looked up at him in surprise and saw a bit of understanding dawning in the man's eyes. His acting had left doubts. Jacob knew he had to do something fast or he'd find himself chained into the same line and heading to who knew where. He turned to the officer, squared his shoulders and glared at him in his best attempt at a superior stare and an evil look.

N
W — 70 — E
S

"I think you better just load these slaves onto the ships and stop wasting good hard workers. I don't think Master Cain would appreciate the loss of good slaves for . . . amusement," Jacob roared into the man's face. He was rewarded with a surprised look and a quick nod of the man's head.

"Yes, sir! Sorry, sir. I . . . I spoke out of turn. Sorry, sir."

"Good. Now get out of here!"

He watched as they moved the line of prisoners down the hill until they finally disappeared from view. Once the street was clear of the column, a few doors opened here and there along the dirty line of huts. A few heads popped out until the locals were sure that the area was clear, and then there was an eruption of activity as a crowd of figures only slightly cleaner then the prisoners went about their business. All of them ignored him, so Jacob joined the moving throng and started up the hill to the west. When he finally reached a decent vantage point, he stopped, turned and drew in a sharp breath. Wherever he was, it was no longer the Duluth he knew. The lay of the land was the same as was the great breath of Lake Superior, but the city was gone. In its place was a collection of brown dilapidated buildings, which he thought had once been quaint little cottages tucked into the hillside. Along the shore he counted thirty long docks jutting out into the lake. The water was brown and fouled with debris and filth. The buildings closer to the docks were mainly large warehouse structures but built from wood and stone. The dwellings diminished in stature quickly as they proceeded up the hill.

All around him, the hillside had been stripped of trees, and he could see where great washouts had destroyed entire sections of the hills. The ships pulled into the docks were like nothing he had ever seen. They were massive and box like, almost like the ore carriers that had once plied the lake in droves, but these all had great paddlewheels attached to their sides. Each one also had mounted cannons on the fore and aft decks. A pair of great smoke stacks rose out of the middle of the ships.

"Where am I?" Jacob muttered. "This must be what Tasker was talking about. A world divided from ours but similar in land and bodies of water." When a passerby stopped to stare at him he quickly continued up the hillside.

He found himself standing on a rocky outcropping. The last of the dirty houses lay behind and below his tired footsteps. The sun was setting, and the last rays of light made a brilliant display against the clouds of smog and smoke.

The tolling of several bells that echoed across the hillside caused a scurry of people rushing to their houses. He heard the report of doors closing all over. He scratched his head and suddenly noticed a small form staring at him from a thick stand of brush.

"It's curfew time you know."

"I . . ." Jacob was at a loss of what to say.

"I saw the way you spoke to those soldiers. You're not one of them are you?" The voice was gentle and sounded female.

Jacob squinted trying to get a good look at the person who was speaking to him, but the figure was all but invisible against the shadows under the thick brush. All he could see for sure was a pair of luminescent eyes that bore into him without blinking. That stare seemed to lay his soul bare.

"Is it that obvious?" he asked finally. "I don't even know where I am." Jacob slumped to the ground and drew his knees up to his chest, he would have had a hard time admitting it had his friends been there, but he was feeling alone, tired, and more than a little scared. This was not what he had envisioned when Jane texted him and asked him to come over earlier that night.

There was a rustle in the brush before him, and he saw a small figure emerge from the brush and flex a pair of silky wings. She came about up to his knees but was perfectly proportioned and amazingly beautiful. He watched spell bound as she flapped her wings and rose into the air in front of him. She took his face in a tiny pair of hands that softly raised his head as she looked into his eyes.

"You can't give up hope. A world without hope is not a world worth saving, and I believe our world is still worth saving."

"What are you?" Jacob asked suddenly.

"I'm a fairy," she replied. "I'm called Bella by my family . . . I do hope some of them has survived."

"What do you mean survived?" Jacob asked. He watched as she fluttered to the ground next to him and sat down with her legs drawn up, mimicking his pose.

"Cain and the Adherents have captured many of my kin and caged them. It's considered a social symbol among their people to own a fairy. They cage us like animals," Bella said in a small voice.

Suddenly Jacob's problems didn't seem so large, and yet, at the same time, his current situation had gotten even more desperate. He saw the small tears fall from her eyes and strike the ground. Each time a tear hit the ground, a small flower grew up almost instantly.

"We need to leave this place," Bella said suddenly. She fluttered off the ground and reached to his hand. "Come with me. We will find you a place that is safe."

Jacob reached out and let her place her small fingers on his index finger. She pulled him along towards the wall of underbrush, and they entered the thicket.

CHAPTER EIGHT
Help Me

JANE STARED IN SHOCK AT THE FLOOR where just the moment before Jacob had laid to reach under her bed. He was gone, simply gone. She saw no signs of where he was or even that he had ever been there. She stumbled backwards and fell over the chair with a crash that nearly broke the small writing desk pushed up against the wall.

"Jany, are you all right?" a voice echoed up the steps. There was a creaking of stairs as her grandfather started up the steps.

She hurried to the door and managed to smile down at him and say, "Yes, I'm fine, Grandpa. I just slipped."

"Okay," Grandpa Able nodded to her and returned to the living room where he was watching the news.

She slipped the door shut with her foot and scuttled over to look under the bed. The emblem was also gone.

"Jacob!" she hissed as thought saying his name might bring him back from wherever he was hiding. Her mind swirled with thoughts of where could he have gone, how his disappearance was like the black-robed man's, what she possibly could do now. Finally her mind latched onto one thing and repeated it to her over and over. There was only one person who could help her and that was Tasker. She had to find the little man wherever he was hiding. What was it he had said to her? Align the crystals, that was it, align the crystals, and he would try to come to her.

She fumbled about until she found the compass through her tears. She clutched the instrument and crawled back until

N
W ⊲74⊳ E
S

she was huddled in the corner with the bat gripped in one hand the compass in the other. The window was still locked shut, and her door was closed but the latch was open. The house around her was silent. When the clock on her nightstand said eleven, she slowly put down the bat and managed to dry her eyes. The compass lay silently in her hand waiting for her to decide what to do.

"All right. Here it goes." Jane picked up her phone from where it fallen on the floor and slipped it into her pocket. She felt she was ready to try to summon the mysterious Tasker.

The crystals on the top of the compass were separated into three distinct areas and a single line crossed through the entire surface. Carefully she grasped the outer ring and turned it until it was straight up and down. With that accomplished, she carefully pushed on the middle ring and found that it moved easily under the pressure of her finger. As the dial moved, Jane felt the effects of the movement shudder through the room around her, as though the movement of the dial was rotating the world around her slightly. The moment the ring lined up with the outer one, the shaking affect faded. She put her finger on the last ring and spun it quickly to line up with the others. This time the weird feelings that had happened were much less, and she was able to shake them off quickly.

"Well, what now," Jane muttered. She stared darkly at the compass and ground her teeth. *Where is the little man. Why doesn't he just appear immediately?*

She sat on the edge of her bed, clutching the bat while she waited. If only there was someone she trusted close by, but Jacob was gone and her grandpa would not understand what was going on. He'd probably call the police and file a report on a disappearing attacker. Then her mom would find out and promptly freak out, and Jane would probably be back in the

Twin Cities before she could find out what happened to Jacob and Jacky. Suddenly she heard a small scratching at the window, and raised her bat and huddled carefully in the corner. When the sounds at the window continued, she finally scooted out into the room just far enough to glance quickly at the glass. The face behind the glass was not one of the sinister black-robed men.

"Tasker," Jane muttered. She nodded as the little man waved frantically to her. "I'm coming," she said and scrambled to her feet. She tossed the bat on the bed and walked to the window. She flipped the two latches and slid the window open. "It's about time you got here."

CHAPTER NINE
Jacob Is in My World

TASKER REACHED UP FROM WHERE he balanced on top of an overturned patio chair and grabbed her hand, he was too short to reach the window ledge without help and so was forced to let Jane pull him over the edge. Every rough edge in the wood tore at him, trying to slow him but he scrambled with his feet and finally managed to worm half way into the room.

"Oomph!"

Jane winced when her grip on the little man slipped and he was stuck half way in the window and half out, his legs wiggling wildly. "Hold on," she said. She grabbed his flailing arms and gave a good hard pull. With a tumble of legs and arms they both fell to the floor eliciting a groan from Jane as the thump sounded throughout the house.

"What happened?" Tasker started. He stood and looked around the room.

"Shh," Jane hissed. "I don't want my grandparents coming up here and try to find out what's going on." She walked to the door, opened it, and stepped out into the short hall that separated her room from the bathroom and the stairs leading down to the main floor. There was the sound of shuffling feet below but they stopped as the bathroom light clicked on and the door swung shut. The television blared. Thankfully it had drowned out the clatter of noise.

"I think it's all right," Jane muttered when she entered her room again to find Tasker sitting cross legged on the edge of the bed. She opted for the chair and slumped down in it across from him.

"What happened?" Tasker repeated.

"One of those guys, what are they called?" Jane asked as her mind tried to penetrate the fog that lack of sleep was bringing on. "The ones in the black robes."

"Adherents," Tasker prompted. "Messengers and spies sent by Cain to this side of the Divide."

"Whatever," Jane cut him off. "One of them tried to break into my room about two hours ago." She checked the time on her watch and confirmed. "I hit him on the head with my bat while he wasn't looking."

"Where is he?" Tasker said suddenly, as he leapt to his feet and looked about.

"That's just it, he disappeared," Jane muttered. She reached up and rubbed her eyes trying to get rid of the tiredness that seemed to be seeping out of every pore of her mind and body.

"Was he wearing a little red metal emblem or medallion?" Tasker asked. He looked around on the floor as if hoping to find the medallion close by. "Oh, this would be a great thing if we were able to take one of Cain's few medallions."

"Well, yes, he had one, but when I pulled it off he disappeared," Jane sputtered as she tried to interrupt his ramblings. "It rolled under the bed."

"Did you touch it?" Tasker asked immediately as he bent down and looked under the bed. "I don't see it."

"No. It fell under the bed. I couldn't reach it. Jacob reached under the bed to grab it, and he disappeared," Jane said.

Tasker stopped his fumbling under the bed and looked up at her from the floor. He sighed and muttered, "Can things go more wrong for me? Now the boy, who could be the key to this whole mess, has been dumped in Cain's grasp, and I'm stuck here with a map maker who refuses to believe me. Can things get any worse?"

"What are you saying?" asked Jane.

Tasker waved his hand. "The boy has crossed over through the Divide, probably through no effort of his own." Tasker said. "The medallion is a marker tied to a specific map. Unfortunately for your friend, if he managed to activate the marker then he has crossed over into my world."

"How could he activate it if he didn't even know what it was?" Jane protested.

"It doesn't take much if he has natural talent as a runner. Was he wearing the ring I gave him?" Without waiting for an answer Tasker muttered to himself. "Still what are the chances of a true cartographer and a true runner being this close to each other. Such an event has only happened one other time, and that was in a time of great danger . . ." Tasker voice faded and he seemed lost in his own thoughts.

"Yes, I think he had on the ring, but, hello, what is a runner?" Jane said finally when it seemed the little man had completely forgotten about her.

Tasker blinked twice and looked around as though awaking from a dream. "What?" he asked.

"And where exactly *is* Jacob?"

"Jacob is in my world," Tasker replied. "Hopefully he arrived in a place where Cain's Adherents did not find him, and he was able to hide. And, hopefully, he does not run into any of Cain's spies while he is there because if he does it is only a matter of time until they turn him over to Cain. A runner is someone who workers with a map maker. Runners are able to more easily pass between the worlds, almost as easily as in the days before the Divide was raised. Hopefully, he does not try and pass over too often though."

"So if he went there, he can come back, right?" Jane demanded. "What difference does it make how often?" she tacked on as his words sank into her.

"Well, maybe," Tasker hemmed. "You see, I assume when Cain sent his Adherent across the Divide, he planted a return point on the map that was linked to the medallion. If Jacob is not a runner he would not be able to find his way back here with an anchor point, he could be lost in the Divide forever." Tasker hesitated, hoping Jane would not remember the second part of her question. No need to make her more fearful then she already was.

"How do you know all this?" Jane asked finally.

"Because it is the way I would have done it if I was sending someone across to this world."

"But why would this Cain person do what you do?"

"Because," Tasker said with a shake of his head and a sad look in his eyes. "Cain was my student for many years."

"Student?" Jane muttered.

"Yes," Tasker said. "At least three of the maps Cain's used to send his Adherents across into this world, I created along with their medallions. He stole them from me when he left."

"I'm so confused," Jane muttered. "I just want to see if my sister is alive and get Jacob back to this world."

"Look," Tasker said patiently. "Each medallion is linked to a certain map. The medallions give Cain's spies the ability to move between worlds as long as they are in an area covered by the map. In the case of the medallion your friend has, it is a small map centered on this town. I know the map because it is one of mine. I penned the sea monster on it in honor of a creature that has haunted the depths of what you call the Great Lakes for years. I created the medallion to look like the tentacles of a sea creature. Step outside the boundaries of that map and the medallion is worthless. Stay inside the area, and his spies can move across the Divide each time their medallion charges, using both sides of the Divide to reach their goals. Do you understand? That is how the Adherent on the train disappeared from the cars. He simply passed back to his world and waited for his medallion to recharge. A true runner doesn't have to wait for anchors to recharge. He can pass back and forth much more easily."

Jane nodded.

"Jacob doesn't realize it, but he possesses the ability to return here anytime he wants to, if he truly is a runner. The bad thing is that anyone can use a medallion once a day without losing themselves in the Divide. It takes true talent to do it repeatedly. If he isn't a runner, he will be lost forever if he tries to find a way back. The anchor is the only thing that brings Cain's spies back from their missions."

"I think I understand," Jane said finally. "How do we get Jacob back?"

"We have to cross back over," Tasker said.

"But if I go missing, it will kill my mom," Jane muttered. She slumped in her chair, she was more unsure now then she had ever been in her life. "I can't."

"Jane, you must understand that Cain's forces will not stop," Tasker said to her. "He doesn't care how many of his followers he sends on one-way trips through the Divide. He will keep sending them until he manages to bring you through on one of his maps. If he does that, he can bring you straight into a prison cell or surrounded by his Adherents with no chance of escape. If we go through on our own terms, we stand a chance of evading his forces and finding a way to defeat him." He paused for a moment, "And we stand a chance of finding your sister."

Jane grimaced. If there was even the slightest chance of finding her sister and bringing her back than she had to take it. No risk was too great if it meant Jackie would be safe.

"I need to leave a note for my grandpa," Jane said as she rose to her feet. "It'll gain us a day at least before my grandparents call the police."

"Just make it vague," Tasker said. "Remember anything you leave can be found by Cain's trackers and used against us."

Jane nodded as she pulled a sheet of paper from the top drawer of the desk and folded it in half. She wrote a note and slipped downstairs to leave it on the counter. It simply said she was going to drive up the north shore and go hiking for the day with Jacob, and that she would be back late. Hopefully they would not wait up for her. She left the folded paper on the counter next to the coffee maker where her grandpa would find it in the morning. Then she crept back upstairs.

"What do we do?" Jane asked Tasker when she returned to the room. She laid out the compass and the roll of leather he had given her.

"First we need you to start a map," Tasker said. This would be her first test. He would see if she had the ability to create a map of her own without resorting to his. "It doesn't need to be anything elaborate, just recognizable as the area around your house and, preferably, written on something that won't burn easily." He pointed to the roll of material lying on the bed covers. "Open it. I made it for you. It's vellum made in the days before the Divide. It's what the ancients used when they created their maps. There's very little of it left in the world."

"What's vellum?" Jane asked, trying to remember the term.

"Sheep skin, calf skin, a specially prepared type of soft leather," Tasker explained. "It is what most important documents were written on many years ago."

Jane reached out slowly and retrieved the vellum roll. She slid her fingers down to the lead seal and was surprised to find that it slipped open easily. She began unrolling the vellum scroll and was even more surprised to find it was much larger then she thought it would be. All told it was nearly five feet long and a foot wide, wrapped into the middle of the roll was a small medallion that looked like a pen. It was carved of a material that looked like gold, and she noticed that it felt light.

Carefully she laid the medallion where Tasker indicated she should put it, then she retrieved the second item he'd given her, an intricately carved fountain pen.

"All right, this is your first map. More importantly, this is your point of safe return should you ever need it. As long as you have your map, you can always return to this one small map," Tasker explained. "It'll be simple, easy to draw, and anything on this map roll is linked to this medallion. Start with the basic shape of the house. Think about the house as you draw and see it in your mind's eye."

Jane followed his instructions and sketched the exterior of the house, the lines flowing off the pen with an ease that she never felt during art classes in school. When the exterior matched what she saw in her mind, she moved onto the interior without waiting for Tasker to tell her. It took less than ten minutes for the interior of the house to take shape and when she was done, she leaned back and smiled at her handiwork. Tasker leaned over her shoulder and examined it critically.

"It's a good first attempt. It's rough, but I suppose it'll work for now," he muttered with a shake of his head. "Now place the medallion on the edge of the map and sketch an image of it where you are standing. Also, always make sure you define the edges of your map, especially the one that you plan to use as a safe point."

Jane leaned back over the leather and placed the medallion inside the area she had marked off and drew a tiny image of the pen right in the place where her bed was.

"Good," Tasker leaned close to the map and looked at it. He reached inside his own overcoat and pulled out a slightly battered roll of leather and placed it next to hers on the bed. Next he pulled a tiny medallion from an inner pocket and pinned it to his coat. "Let me see here." Tasker unrolled his leather revealing an intricately detailed drawing of the surrounding countryside that made Jane's sketch look like a child's stick figure. "We should be about right here on my map." He etched in a tiny marker that looked like a small mallet. "Listen to me," Tasker said as he looked up at Jane. "When you put the medallion on you are going to pass through without doing anything. The first trip through is always the hardest. You'll be a bit disorientated when you arrive on the far side. Don't let that bother you. I'll find you right away, so don't go looking for me!"

Jane nodded.

"I *will* find you," Tasker repeated. "Now this is important. Whatever you do, keep your medallion and your map hidden and close to you. And above all keep the compass hidden."

"What is the compass for?" Jane asked.

"The compass is an experiment of mine," Tasker said. "Just keep it hidden until we need it and keep changing the dials each day."

She picked the compass up off the bed and fiddled with the dials for a minute until she was sure that each of them had been changed, and then she tucked the bronze compass into the inner pocket of her jacket.

"Let me see your finger," Tasker said suddenly and he held out his hand. He reached down and retrieved the small pen medallion and manipulated the pin open.

Jane reached out to him and jumped when he pricked her finger with the pin and then fastened it to her jacket.

"Ouch! You could have warned me," Jane said accusingly as she put the pricked finger in her mouth and sucked away the drop of blood that welled up.

"Well, the medallion needs a bit of the user's blood," Tasker said with a shrug. "It helps the device work well."

"I . . ." Jane muttered, but suddenly the room began to grow fuzzy and her eyes flickered rapidly, trying to clear the dizziness she felt.

"Don't fight it," Tasker said to her but his voiced seemed far away to her. "Give in to the magic. It will make the transition easier." He watched her fade until she completely disappeared. For the first time in many years, hope blossomed in his heart. With a great smile, he activated his own anchor and started his own trip across the Divide.

TASKER AND HER ROOM vanished, and Jane found herself standing before a great wall of darkness, it pressed against her from all sides. Panic began to set it. She pushed forward trying to move and found that pressing through was similar to wading through mud. She tried turning back but found that way back was blocked. Step after laborious step, she pushed forward until the darkness began to fade. Sudden she felt the world around her right itself and she fell free of the passage and slumped to the ground in the darkness. The moon shone bright overhead, but billows of smoke kept rising from the ground and blocking its light.

"Tasker," she whispered into the darkness but nothing answered her. In the distance she heard a shout of voices, and as her eyes cleared, she found she was sitting in a small clearing. Off to her right was a stone cottage with the windows darkened. The roof was no longer intact and looked as though fire had been used to scorch away the wood used in the construction. Few trees grew on the hillside, and far below her she could see the reddish glow reflecting off a row of great structures near the shores of Lake Superior. Torches lit the decks of a row of great iron ships tied up to wooden piers. Around the ships the darkness was held back by hundreds of torches. The air smelled foul, and she nearly gagged when she breathed deeply. The basic lay of the land was similar to the Duluth she knew, but the buildings were all wrong.

Jane stifled the bout of coughing as best she could. Who knew what lurked in the shadows of this place. A rustling in the brush off to her right drew her attention, and she turned towards it as terror filled her. Why had she done it? Why had she agreed to come here? Her breath came in short gasps. Whatever was moving through the brush came closer and closer.

"Tasker?" she whispered again desperately. Two days ago she would have hardly been happy to see the little man but now she would give anything for his face to appear out of the gloom. The movements in the underbrush grew more and more violent until the thick brambles swayed and moved against the sky's slight paleness. Jane finally found the strength to move away from her approaching doom. She dashed to the dilapidated cottage walls and slipped inside where the door had once been. Crouched behind the wall, she watched as the movements of the brush slowed and the night fell silent. Then she heard the muttering of a familiar voice.

"Stupid thorn weeds," Tasker muttered when he finally emerged from the underbrush. Jane could see him, then, standing at the edge of the clearning. He seemed to be examining his jacket and trying to free it of thorns and twigs clung stubbornly to the cloth. "Jane? Where are you?" Tasker hissed as he looked about the open area before the cottage. He continued tearing the brambles from his jacket.

"I'm here," Jane said as relief flooded through her. She wiped her face with trembling hands and tried to will herself to stop shaking. After a moment, she stood and waved to him. When he spotted her, she slumped again and leaned against the cool stones.

"Why did you move?" Tasker asked accusingly when he slipped into the ruined cottage. "I told you not to move."

"I thought something was coming through the brush, something . . . I don't know, bigger." Jane pointed to the hole in the thicket where he just emerged. "How does a guy your size managed to shake that brush for like ten feet in both directions."

Tasker turned around looked at the brambles for a minute and then he turned back to her with a half-smile on his face. "Point well taken." He looked around at the ruined cottage sadly. It was as he remembered it, still set against the flat-faced cliff where he had built it so many years ago as his last hiding place. It was to here he had fled when he learned of Cain's betrayal. Without the backing of the Northern Committee on Fantastic Creatures, he knew it was only a matter of time until Cain took control of the northern reaches of the world. The other committees ignored his pleas for help and stubbornly insisted that this was a Northern Committee matter, and refused to interfere. He wondered how far Cain's reach had extended in his long absence.

"Come on. We need to get out of the open," Tasker said. He turned to the back of the cottage and approached the flat face of the small cliff. One thing he had done when he fled and that was hide his work place. The wooden shelf had been replaced with a magical door that had taken nearly a year to prepare. No one could open this door but he. Indeed no one could even find it without his aid. It was built that way and linked to the energy fields that surround the earth. The door sensed his approach and the fact that he wished entry and slowly swung open to allow him and Jane entrance to the dark passage beyond. Had he not wished entry, the portal would not have opened and the cliff face would have remained immovable.

Jane followed Tasker into the ruined cottage slowly. She looked down one last time at the city just emerging from night. Somewhere out there her sister could still be alive and frightened out of her mind. Somewhere out there Jacob was trying to survive, and she had to find both of them. Hopefully they could find a way to stop this Cain character in the process so that they and their world would be safe once more.

CHAPTER TEN
Will O' Wisp

B RANCHES CLUTCHED AT JACOB'S clothes, but he noticed with a bit of irritation that they seemed to give
way before Bella. She pulled him along until the
thicker underbrush opened up, and the forest stretched out
before them. It was dark, and the moon only penetrated the
canopy overhead in a few places. Jacob's feet seemed to find
each dip, hillock, and protruding root in the forest floor. The
fourth time he fell, he lay for a moment, his fists clenched.

"Fairy wood," Bella said with a smile at him. "Come. We
cannot stop, not yet."

"I'm tired," Jacob muttered as he leaned against a tree.

"Please, it's not far now," Bella begged. "We can rest once
we arrive."

"Fine. I'm coming," Jacob muttered as he pulled his body
up off the forest floor one last time. They continued on for another half hour before Bella motioned for him to stop. Jacob
knew they were north and west of the city, but he wasn't sure
how far. A small river flowing merrily through a gorge nearby,
and Bella motioned for him to approach the water.

"Just up river is a waterfall," Bella explained. "There's a small
cave behind it. You will just fit inside. If you crawl through the
opening, it'll widen into a bigger room. Wait for me there. I
need to cover our tracks. You left a trail obvious enough for a
blind man to follow." She motioned for him to go.

"Well, excuse me," Jacob muttered as she turned and fluttered away. He watched for a moment and was amazed to see

that the forest seemed to respond to her call. The branches he had broken stumbling along behind her suddenly righted themselves, and areas where he had stepped the grass straightened. He watched wide-eyed until she was out of sight. Then he crawled down the rocky edge of the gorge and made his way up the edge of a small but fast-moving river. He had gone about a hundred yards when arrived at the waterfall. It thundered loudly over a cliff twenty feet high and he wondered how he was supposed to reach the cave behind it. There was one large rock in the middle of the river and he waded out to it, shivering against the cold bite in the water. He stood shaking on the rock for a minute before finally gathering the courage to shove his head through the wall of water and look around.

"There is it," he muttered as the streams of water soaked his head and sent goosebumps across his body. He was used to cold water, but this little river held a bite that he hadn't felt since he jumped into Lake Superior on a dare.

There was a small opening just large enough for him to wiggle into, and he pushed his shoulders in and began using his arms and feet to pull his body through. He had made it fully into the tunnel when his belt caught on something behind him, and his forward movement stopped. Panic began to set in, and he twisted his body back and forth, trying to clear whatever was holding him but failed miserably. He tried to slip his arm around behind his body, but a rock blocked his hand.

"Jacob," Bella called, her tiny voice barely louder than the thunder of the water. "Can you keep moving forward?"

"No. I'm stuck," he called back with more than a bit of frustration in his voice. He had only been stuck in a cave one other time, and the claustrophobia came flooding back to him in a moment. There were many underwater caverns and caves along the edges of Lake Superior, and he and a friend had found an entrance to one that was only half submerged. They swam in on the hottest day of the summer hoping that the water would be warm enough for them to reach the interior. Jacob still remembered when he emerged from the swim and found that the cloth of his swim suit was caught just under the surface. Thankfully his friend had been wearing his dive knife. After a quick cut, he was once again floating free, minus half his swimsuit.

"Hold on," Bella said. "Don't move. I'm going to see if I can free you."

"All right," Jacob muttered as he forced the panic out of his voice. He felt a bit of moment as the little fairy moved by his legs, then a tickle of movement as she reached his back.

"Your belt's caught," Bella muttered. "I'm going to cut it."

Jacob waited until she was clear, then continued pulling through the tunnel. Without his belt to hold his pants in place, he was soon crawling with his trousers half way down to his knees. "This is embarrassing," Jacob muttered as he finally fell free of the tunnel and looked about in wonder. A half a dozen more fairies fluttered around the cavern, and they all looked at him in surprise. Shouts of warning arose. Then Bella emerged from the tunnel and flew up to where the rest were gathering.

"Wait, wait."

Jacob could hear her calling for calm as he pulled his pants back up around his waist and examined his severed belt. The leather was a complete loss, but as long as he was not forced to run or do anything too active he would be fine. Too much activity, and he would have to hold his pants up with one hand.

The cavern where he was standing was at least twenty feet across and he thought maybe twice that deep. The ceiling was fairly level as it went out from the entrance, but the floor fell away to a pool of clear water, and he suddenly realized how thirst he was.

"Bella," Jacob called as he made his way down the slope to the pool of water. "Can I have a drink?" He pointed down at the water. Suddenly he noticed a point of light rising from the water towards him.

"Yes," she called back to him and then turned back to the animated conversation she was having with the other fairies.

Jacob stood by the pool looking down for a minute, trying to decide what was hidden in its depths. A glowing ball of light floated up through the depths, making him a bit more scared and a little less thirsty. When it finally erupted from the water, the ball filled the cavern with light.

"Greetings, human."

Jacob stumbled back and fell to the ground as a sphere of light about the size of his fist spoke to him. His eyes grew wide and he pressed his body back against the ground, wondering what in the world was hovering before him.

"Uh, hello?" he finally muttered.

"The water is cool and refreshing. You should drink."

"All right," Jacob managed to whisper. He leaned out over the pool and dipped some of the water up with his hand. The creature floating near him was right. The water was cool and it tasted better than anything he had ever had before. When he had slaked his thirst, he looked up at the creature.

"Just for curiosity," Jacob asked as politely as he could. "What are you?"

"In some places, I'm known as a will o' wisp. Other cultures have called me a spirit, but that's hardly accurate."

"I read a book once that talked about jack o lanterns," Jacob sputtered. "But I thought that was all fairy tales."

"Some say that all tales have at least a small part of their story based in reality," the will o' wisp said softly. "My kind have been around since the beginning of humankind and some of my kin were not always the nicest."

The will o' wisp seemed to have said all it was going to say. Jacob watch in fascination as it dipped back into the water and dwindled until it was gone, and the cavern was once again bathed in dimness.

"Jacob," Bella floated down to where he stood and smiled at him. Her features were fine and a small smile danced around her lips as she spoke. "We've decided that you'll be allowed to stay here for the night at least. You'll be given a place to sleep and food to eat. Tomorrow we must decide what to do. You are not meant to be here, and yet I sense there's a reason you're here."

The water seemed to have made Jacob drowsy, and he nodded to her, unsure what else he could do. He heard the soft sound of singing voices in the background. Suddenly Jacob realized he was lying on a bed of soft moss. The cavern had grown warmer, his clothes drier, and his eyes slipped slowly shut. The last thing he heard as his mind slipped off to sleep was, "This is it," a voice said. "This is the way to free our kin."

"It's wrong," Bella retorted. "How do we know he will keep his end of the bargain?"

"We don't, but we have to trust if we're going to flee this place as a family."

"I still think it's wrong," Bella repeated. "He's done nothing to us, and we're going to betray him."

Jacob tried to raise his hand towards the voices but then everything faded to black, and he slept.

JANE AWOKE WITH A START and looked around, it had been dark last night when they entered Tasker's workshop. He had shown her to an alcove that contained a sleeping area, and she had fallen asleep almost immediately. The room where she lay was still dark but beyond a curtain was ample light. She heard the rustle of cloth and instruments as Tasker moved about his workshop.

Jane shuffled to her feet and stretched, feeling well-rested for the first time in more than three days. After retrieving her jacket and making sure everything was still in place, she pushed back the curtain and walked out into Tasker's workshop. The short man was standing before a table leaning over a leather-bound volume nearly as thick as his head. He looked up when she entered.

"Ah, Jane," Tasker said with a smile. "I hope your sleep left you well-rested?"

"Surprisingly, yes," Jane admitted. "I normally don't sleep that well outside my own room."

"We have a busy day today," Tasker replied. "I'm starting to become worried about Jacob and where he's gotten off to. After you fell asleep, I went out for a walk to see if I could track him down, but his trail went cold at the edge of the Fairy wood."

"And what is that?" Jane asked. So many strange things had been thrown at her in the last couple of days that a strangely named forest didn't even faze her, only made her curious.

"Well, it's where a local family of fairies took up residence when they left Ireland," Tasker replied with a shrug of his shoulders. "I'm sorry. I thought the name was self-explanatory." He turned away from her and continued to fiddle with the items laid out on the table before him.

Jane narrowed her eyes at him, but her stomach growled. Instead of starting an argument, she looked around for food. "Is there anything to eat in this world?" Her sarcasm seemed lost on Tasker, who simply pointed to where a half of a loaf of bread and a slice of cheese lay at the end of the table.

"I picked that up in town from the local baker. He still remembered me and offered his help."

"Right," Jane muttered as she walked to the small table that held the food.

"Help yourself," he muttered and then returned to his book. "It's a problem Jacob went there because fairies possess a good bit of skill in working with nature. It may take me an hour or two to find out where they took him."

"What would fairies want with Jacob?" Jane asked around a mouthful of food. The bread was good, if a bit dry, but the cheese was the best she had ever tasted. There was a clay jar of water sitting on the table, and she sipped from it as she ate.

"Well, most likely to try to trade him for their kin." Tasker said with an uncomfortable squirm. "Cain has broken many rules in his time in power. One of them is to allow the hunting and capturing of naturally intelligent creatures by the dominant humanoid races."

"Humanoid?" Jane asked curiously. "What do you mean, they're different than humans?"

"All sorts of them—elves, dwarves, goblins, and a dozen others. Added to that are many creatures here that have intelligence, some greater than others. But they lack the sheer numbers to stop the Adherents from taking advantage of them. Well, except for a few of the larger races that no one in his right mind would try to capture. I've yet to see a dragon brought down in chains," Tasker explained. He chuckled out of the side of his mouth, "Too bad we're not all dragons."

"So what do we do?" Jane asked as she put a piece of cheese on a bit of bread and popped it into her mouth.

"This sounds like the perfect time to use your new abilities," Tasker said with a smile. "What better way to learn."

Jane rolled her eyes and groaned, "Great. First day here and I get a pop quiz."

"Come, it won't be anything too difficult," Tasker promised. "We'll talk as we walk to the forest."

The sun was shining beyond the cloud of smog that hung over the city when they emerged from the underground tunnel. Jane noticed that, although the cottage was still mostly ruins, the roof had been repaired, and the door reattached to its hinges. She had no idea when Tasker had had time for this.

The small clearing around the cottage was quiet, and Tasker looked about as he slid the door open just a bit. When he saw nothing nearby, he motioned her out of the tunnel and slid the door shut.

They moved north, leaving the filthy city behind and entering an area still filled with forests and undergrowth. Ferns grew in abundance, and all type of flowers mixed into the few meadows competing for the sunlight. They had walked for about thirty minutes when Tasker called a halt atop a small hill. In the distance was a small river that went over a pair of stair step falls with the highest drop being about twenty feet.

Suddenly Tasker grabbed Jane, and pulled her down beside him behind a rock that jutted out of the ground. He put a finger across his lips.

"What is it?" Jane whispered as she brushed the dirt off her jeans.

"Trackers," Tasker muttered. He pointed down to where the biggest of the falls cascaded over the rocks and dropped into a wide pool. Creeping along the back of the river were two men, both wearing black robes. "No medallions though. That's good," Tasker said as he watched them from around the corner of their shelter.

"Quickly," Tasker instructed, "put your map down on the ground here. Sketch out the river bed."

Jane dropped to her knees again and unrolled her map roll. She took the pen and began sketching the banks of the river as she sneaked quick looks down the hill.

"Good enough," Tasker muttered. "Look, you have to get to that tracker and do it quickly. You see where he's hidden on the far side of the river?"

Jane glanced over the edge of the rock and marked his position on the map before her, she nodded.

"Maps in the right hands can do more than just allow travel between worlds," Tasker hurriedly explained. "In the hands of a true cartographer, what's drawn on the map can come to happen in the world. A word of warning, however, what happens in one world happens in the other, except in the case of the most skilled of cartographers. And it's temporary. Sometimes things will last for minutes before reverting to the true form. Sometimes changes may last for a day, but nothing can be changed permanently."

Jane stared at him, realizing what he was saying for the first time, "So this Cain has a magic map of Lake Superior. What he draws on it happens in both worlds?"

"He wiped out a section of the city on this world when he struck at you in your world," Tasker confirmed. "A good thing to keep in mind before you start changing things."

"What he did seems pretty permanent," Jane said.

"Nothing done to the land or the water was permanent. That does not hold true to things that mortals have added," Tasker replied.

"What do I do?" Jane said.

"Should be nothing wrong with expanding the river just a little," Tasker suggested to her. "It'll serve our purpose and revert to normal quickly."

Jane looked at the etchings of the river on her map and wondered what was about to happen back in her world. Would someone be near the river and be swept away?

"We have to do it now, Jane," Tasker said. He pointed down the hill to where a group of floating figures had emerged from the waterfall. Wrapped in a glowing net was the still form of Jacob, who seemed to be sleeping peacefully.

"Uh oh. Trouble," Tasker muttered. "It looks like Cain's trackers are getting ready to double-cross the fairies." He pointed up river where two more men were creeping along the river bank with closely woven nets in their arms. "I'll take care of the ones on top of the waterfall. You just concentrate on the ones below." Tasker bent over his own map and began sketching as fast as his hands could move across his map.

Jane nodded and then looked down at her map. With sure strokes she expanded the river bed under where two of the men were hiding. When that was done, she added a few stones and curls to make it seem like the river was raging across its banks. She glanced up when she was done and stared in amazement as the river suddenly surged over its banks, and the ground dropped out from under two of the trackers, leaving them struggling in the water. Moments later they were both washed downstream and disappeared under the rush of water. Up river Jane could see the other two ambushers struggling against a widening sink hole of mud that finally sucked them into its depths.

"Good. Your changes are already fading from the world," Tasker muttered under his breath. He pointed to where the land was rising back up out of the river, and the water was once again flowing slowly out of the pool below the falls.

Jane looked around the edge of the boulder again but there was no sign of the trackers anywhere. The fairies, however, were staring up the hillside and seemed to know exactly where they were hiding.

"What happened to the trackers?" Jane asked but she was not really sure she wanted to hear the answer."

"They are not permanent parts of the landscape. They are lost somewhere in the Divide now I would think

"Tasker, what are those?" Jane pointed to the floating creatures who were carrying the still form of Jacob between them.

"Those my dear are fairies," Tasker said as he tucked his map away. "Gather up your things, and we'll go deal with the little creatures that just about got the rest of their family captured."

CHAPTER ELEVEN
Deal with the Devil

I TOLD YOU IT WAS A BAD IDEA," Bella shouted. The other fairies hung their heads in shame and refused to look up at her. Finally one of them spoke.

"But how do we get the rest of our family back?"

"You don't deal with Cain's Adherents. They'll lie to you every time." Bella pointed up the hill. "If it weren't for the dwarf, none of us would be here anymore. We'd all be locked in a cage waiting to be sent downriver." She shook her fist in the face of one of the fairies and glared at him.

As they argued, Tasker and Jane had come down to the river bank. Tasker looked at her and narrowed his eyes, "That will be enough of that, my dear." He glanced back at Jane and then looked at Jacob, who was still sleeping peacefully in his enchanted net. "If you would please release the boy, we'll go someplace safer to talk. I'd rather not stay where the Adherents may come to look for their lost trackers."

Jane leaned over Jacob's sleeping form and pulled the net back from his face. He looked peaceful as he lay on the ground in the middle of a bed of green grass. Carefully she cleared the net from his whole body and then shook his shoulder.

"Jacob?" Jane said and was awarded with the flutter of his eyes. She called his name again and shook his shoulder once more. This time he sat up, a confused look on his face.

"Where am I?" Then his voice trailed off as the memories of the last few night flooded back to him. "Never mind. I remember. I also distinctly remember a short floating fairy who

N
W ◄(100)► E
S

said she was going to keep me safe." He looked around at the net lying on the ground and then up at Bella accusingly.

"Not now, son," Tasker muttered. He motioned for them to follow him and turned up river. "Your cave isn't safe anymore. The trackers could have told others. The chances are next time they'll come with more of their fellows and more dangerous weapons then just nets. Next time the girl and I won't be able to protect you without causing more damage than we can fix. I suggest you come with us for now."

Without waiting to see if they would obey, he started trudging up the river into the thicker forests that blanketed the rolling hills. They walked for some time, and Jane was starting to get tired when Tasker finally called a halt in the middle of a small clearing. The fairies fluttered to the ground and sat with hanging heads, except for Bella, who glared down at her kin with a wrath that only a two-foot-tall fairy could muster.

Jane examined her from the side while they waited for Tasker to sort out what they were going to do. She was beautiful with high cheeks and big round eyes that seemed to draw a person in to their dark depths. The wings sprouting from her back were shimmering, almost translucent, and they moved continuously to keep her hovering. One thing struck Jane as odd was that the fairies' clothing seemed to be made of small leaves stitched together. She reached out and touched the hem of the leaf-dress. Bella looked and her and smiled.

"There was a time when the fairy folk could take bits of sunlight and weave them with the finest silks for our dresses. Now we wear leaves sewn together with strands of spider webs," Bella said quietly, a note of melancholy in her voice. She smoothed her leafy dress sadly and looked down at it. "How the crafty have fallen. All of the knowledge that has been lost since Cain and his Adherents started their cleansing. Some have tried to speculate why Cain's doing what he's doing, but I think he it's because he can, because no one has had the courage or skill to stop him."

She fluttered close to Jane and looked deep into her eyes. "Please help us. My people are dying or captured and those that remain are forced to live in caves and move only under the darkness of night outside those last few sanctuaries. We can't survive like that. The fairy folk need to feel the light of the sun on our faces. We need to be able to dance in the sunlight without fear of nets being cast over us or being locked in cages." There were tears in both Bella's eyes and Jane's as the fairies voice faded to a whisper.

"Look at me," Tasker said suddenly to the four downcast fairies sitting on the ground. "I know you want your family back, but dealing with Cain isn't possible. He'll stab you in the back every time. We tried it, remember? Try to remember why we moved north. It was to avoid the conflicts with him and his Adherents, but it failed. They told us if we moved north would be left alone. Were we? No. Within a few years they followed us here too."

The four small faces looked up at Tasker with tears streaked across the cheeks. They were beaten. Even Jane and Jacob could tell that by looking at their faces. They were a people who had lost all hope.

"How do we stop him?" Jane asked suddenly. Despite what she had been through, she still harbored hope, not only for the freedom and safety of these creatures but also the hope that her sister still survived. If rescuing her sister meant defeating this Cain fellow, then she would do her best to stop him.

"We need allies," Tasker muttered. "There are still lands that have not fallen under Cain's sway. There are still places that may hold strength enough to challenge him. It is in those places we must seek aid. However there are things that may be done here as well. Despite what he believes, Cain has not stamped out all of his opposition even here in what was the crown of the north, Duluth. There are scattered bands of resistance across much of Wiscon as well, but they lack a unified goal. With Cain safe behind the walls of his fortress at Manitoulin Island, we can't touch him. Raising an army to attack such a well-fortified place would be suicide. But if we were to take some of the outer fortresses and watch posts, he'd be forced to respond. Right now we're no more effective than mosquitos stings. We never cause any serious damage. But if we were to bring forces together and launch a coordinated attack, the tiny stings of those mosquitos would suddenly become significant enough that Cain would have to deal with us personally."

"You're talking about something that's going to take weeks to months to set up," Jane protested suddenly. "I can't stay here that long. I need to find my sister and get home before my mom finds out I'm missing."

All eyes turned on her and Jacob. Then Bella said, "We don't need many allies right now. We need one powerful ally, and we need to strike at the place where Cain thinks his power in the northwest is most secure and where we gain the most from attacking him."

"You're talking about the Prison Islands," Tasker said softly. "You know they're protected by a fleet of warships and garrisoned by nearly a thousand of his troops."

"And how many are held captive there?" Bella responded.

"No one knows," Tasker admitted. "Most likely thousands. At least there's room for that many there. Still who would be powerful enough to help us attack them there?"

"You know who I am talking about, Tasker. Everyone but those two knows exactly who I'm speaking of," Bella said quietly. "And you know what price he'll ask for his aid. After all, he's offered his help before, but the cost was considered too high. We need to ask ourselves if we think the price is still too high. Is our continued survival worth that price?"

Tasker was silent for such a long time that Jane finally looked at Bella for an explanation. "Who exactly are you talking about?" she asked finally, exchanging confused looks with Jacob.

"The folk, both human and magical, of this world are watched over—however loosely—by different committees based on where they're located. We were watched over by the Northern Committee on Fantastic Creatures. Alternately in this area it was a subcommittee called the Northern Lakes Committee. The committees have forbidden any from helping this individual because of his behavior."

Jane and Jacob nodded together as they glanced at each other and shrugged. They waited for the explanation to continue. So many strange and wonderful things had been shown to them in the last few days that all they could do was accept what was told to them and keep moving.

"But there are more than just good beings in this world. When the Divide was created, all the mischievous creatures were sent here as well. One of them has a sizable following in the woods to the north of here. The forests stretch for days in all directions, and when no one else seemed to want the lands, he moved his people there, and they have thrived."

"That's an understatement," Tasker muttered. "That the goblins multiplied like rabbits is closer to the truth. Besides the Sealy Council forbids any of the committees from dealing with him."

"That hardily makes a difference anymore. They have refused all your requests since you left their ranks." Bella retorted. "Anyway, this character once controlled all the iron and the mining of it in the northern reaches, but Cain and his forces drove them away. He wants control of the iron back and that is what he asks in return for his help."

"Iron. That's all you're worried about? Control of a few iron mines. That doesn't seem like that big of a thing," Jane said to Tasker.

"It may not to you, but iron is a precious thing in this world. It's poison to some and a building material to others. It has the ability to bind the magical power of most beings, which is how a man such as Cain has managed to stop so many who should have overpowered him," Tasker muttered. "He has control of the iron trade and a steady supply of those willing to follow his command without considering the damage they do to the world around them."

"But my sister could be alive and being held prisoner," Jane shouted suddenly as she snapped inside. Her voice tore through the forest like a bolt of thunder scattering a flight of birds that went winging south.

"Girl, many people's sisters are being held captive, as well as brothers, mothers, fathers, uncles, aunts, *and* children," Tasker responded almost as loudly. "Your sister's been gone for a year. Some of us . . ." he paused. "Well, for some of us it's been a lot longer."

"But if there's a chance of saving so many—" Jacob broke in.

"Would you cut a deal with the devil to save a saint?" Tasker asked him with a piercing look. "I'm not saying we haven't reached that point at the moment. I'm just pointing out that whatever deal we cut to rescue those held captive will be twisted, and we may find ourselves forced into a worse corner in the future." He stood and faced them all. "This is it then. If you wish it, I'll arrange the meeting. God help us if we fail."

"From what I understand, Tasker, there's no other way," Jane said pleadingly. She could see her sister's face in her mind. How badly she wanted to hug her again and tell her how much she missed her.

"I'll arrange the meeting for tonight," Tasker said. "In the mean time, we should prepare. I think you and Jacob should return to your world and reassure your relatives as best you can and find a reason that you can be gone for a day or two if possible. Jane, you have your anchor for this world and can return whenever you wish. Mark this place on your map and return here tonight when the moon rises." He stopped and reached into an inner pocket of his overcoat and brought out a medallion that looked similar to Jane's except slightly smaller. He walked to Jacob and held out his hand to him. When Jacob reached out, he pricked his finger, drawing a yelp of surprise and a snort of laughter from Jane, who had guessed it was coming.

"You could have warned me you were going to do that," Jacob said accusingly to the little man. He sucked at the drop of blood that welled up from his finger and glared down at the little man.

"I find it easier to just prick people when they aren't expecting it," Tasker said with a sly smile. He reached up and pinned the medallion to Jacob's shirt. "This medallion is linked to Jane's map as long as you are in the area covered by her map. You can return here without being lost in the Divide. Focus on your home now and touch the front of the medallion. The power in the device will do the rest. Oh, and, Jacob, keep the ring on."

"Why?' Jacob muttered as he glared down at Tasker.

"It'll keep you safe better than anything else."

"How close are we to our houses?" Jane asked Tasker.

"Not far," he said. When I led you into the woods, I was circling to the south, we should be very close to the edge of what was marked on local maps in your world as the North-land Country Club. By the way," Tasker asked curiously. "What is a country club?"

"It's a place where people play golf," Jacob replied. Then stopped. "I'll explain golf some other time, but it's a game people on our side play." He reached out to Jane and took her hand, pulling her to her feet.

"That way," Tasker pointed. "Bella will guide you to where the map of your house begins. Be back here tonight. I'll meet you when the moon rises at my old cottage. There are some things there that I'll need."

Jane nodded. She and Jacob followed the floating fairy into the woods and began walking back towards the shores of Lake Superior hidden beyond the forest. They walked for some time in silence, but Jane noticed that Jacob held tightly to her hand the entire time, and she liked that fact. It made her feel a bit more secure. Bella seemed happy and animated for the first time since they had met. She moved about with the excited movements of a hummingbird.

"I can't believe he's finally agreed to ask Puck and the goblins for help," Bella squeaked happily. She zipped back to where they were walking and smiled widely at both of them. "This is so exciting."

"Is this Puck really that bad?" Jacob ventured. He had a hard time not smiling at the little fairy.

"Well the goblins aren't really evil, I don't think, more just self-serving. They like playing pranks on people and, well, I guess sometimes people get hurt and they don't seem to care about that but . . ." Bella said but her voice faltered. "The point is that they have the power to help us. They're one of the few groups that Cain hasn't turned his sights on yet. There are entire tribes of goblins living in the northern forests that could be here in a matter of days to help us, and that doesn't include those trolls and giants that Puck could send to help. There are always a few undead types near graveyards they could raise, I suppose, if Tasker asks them to, but the undead are a bit harder to send back once you raise them."

"How can Tasker contact this Puck character?" Jane asked as they broke through the trees and looked down once again at the dirty city of Duluth. They came out of the forest only a dozen paces from Tasker's old cottage, and she hurriedly unrolled her map to make sure they were inside the confines of it. It looked like they were, so she started concentrating on her world and raised her hand to the medallion as Jacob did the same thing.

"Concentrate on our world," Jane said to him. "It felt like I was pushing through a wall of darkness last time, but if you keep moving, you should pop out the far side."

Bella hovered in front of her face. "It's because Tasker was once a friend of his, but there was a horrible battle between the two sides. Much of his family died to the battle . . . but that's old history." Bella twitched her hair. "I'm sure no one's still holding a grudge over that. Well, then there was the time Tasker accused Puck of taking his treasure, but that was never proven either. And then there was the time . . ."

Bella's voice began to fade as Jane touched her medallion. Moments later she was pushing through the veil of darkness and stumbling out onto a fresh-mowed green on the golf course of the country club.

"WELL THAT WAS EASIER," Jacob said as he appeared next to her.

Jane nodded but as she opened her mouth to speak, a sprinkler suddenly erupted from the ground, and a stream of water launched over her head, showering droplets across both of them.

They both jumped in surprise as the cool liquid rained down around them. And then another sprinkler popped up nearby, adding to the torrent. Jane took off running for the edge of the golf course with Jacob sprinting right behind her. They were less than two blocks from her grandparents' house, and soon were out of reach of the sprinklers and walking down the street still holding hands and laughing at each other. Bits of water still dribbled down their necks and left trails across their clothes.

"What if there are more of the trackers?" Jacob asked suddenly. The happy mood extinguished at the thought. He looked around, wondering if anyone was watching them.

"We should keep our windows and doors locked, get some rest because it sounds like the meeting will take place tonight," Jane replied. "What are you going to tell your mom?"

"Nothing," Jacob muttered as he hunched his shoulders some. "She won't even worry about me until I have been gone for a couple of days. She figures I went to a friend's house and forgot to call."

Jane frowned, "I have to think up something to keep my grandpa and grandma from calling the police or worse my mom. They'll never understand that I think there's a chance to get my sister back."

They stopped in front of Jane's grandparents' home and talked for a few more minutes, laying plans and agreeing on a meeting time and then parted. Jane walked up the front steps and cringed as she opened the door.

"Where you been, girl?" Grandpa Able asked the moment she walked in. "And why are you all wet?"

"Jacob and I went for a walk this morning at the country club and got caught by the sprinklers," Jane replied with a forced smile. We weren't' planning on that. We were forced to run through the brush to get out of the water." She continued as she looked down the bedraggled appearance of her clothes. "I'm going to go clean up."

"All righty then," Grandpa Able replied with a shake of his head. "Oh, by the way some guy in a weird outfit stopped by the morning and asked to speak with you. I sent him packing though. Didn't like the look of him in the black robe getup. I told him you had gone back to your mom's house, and he got all mad."

Jane froze at the bottom of the steps. The trackers had been here already, and she was willing to bet they would return quickly now that they knew she was home. They would have someone watching the house, for sure. How was she going to meet with Jacob and return through the Divide while keeping Cain's killers away from her grandparents?

"Grandpa, Jacob asked me to go up to Gooseberry Falls and go hiking, tomorrow. We're going to leave early before the sun rises. I just wanted you to know so you don't worry," Jane turned slowly, hoping her grandfather would not question too closely. She hatedlying to him, but what choice did she have?

"Ah," Grandpa Able said with a wide smile. "You're getting to like him, aren't you? He's such a nice boy. I just knew you two would do well together."

"Grandpa, we're just going hiking," Jane replied with a shake of her head. "It isn't as if he wants to marry me or anything."

"Not yet anyway," Grandpa Able said with an even bigger smile. He turned back to his book and kept chuckling while Jane disappeared up the steps and to shower. "That is how it started with your grandma," he called after her.

CHAPTER TWELVE
Watchers

J ANE STAYED INSIDE MUCH of the afternoon, exchanging texts with Jacob. He agreed he'd come to her house. They would leave directly from her bedroom rather risk being seen leaving the house. No one had yet tried to kidnap him, and he felt reasonably safe that they were more interested in Jane because she had the compass, than he.

Just come for supper.
K what time?
6 good?
Sure.

With that settled, Jane finished putting her hair in a tight ponytail and then hurried down the stairs to the kitchen where her grandmother was slowly arranging dishes on the table. There was a pot of soup simmering on the stove, and she helped arrange the table and put out an extra place setting for Jacob.

"I invited Jacob to eat with us, Grandma," Jane explained as she put down the extra bowl. "I hope you don't mind. His mom's working late I guess."

"That poor boy," Grandpa Able muttered when he walked into the kitchen, which was attached to the dining room. "She's always working late, and he normally eats alone. How he managed to grow up straight eating pizzas and drinking pop constantly is more than I can understand."

It was five after six when Jacob knocked on the front door, and Jane pulled it open for him. "You're late," she hissed with a straight face. Then she smiled at him as the excitement of the coming day flooded over her. She couldn't help but feel a grand adventure was about to begin.

Jacob smiled, "There're watching me now too." He jerked a finger over his shoulder to where a van was parked across the street from his house. "I saw one of the trackers get into the van with a Domino's pizza."

Suddenly Jane smiled to herself and laughed as an idea occurred to her. "I think we can do something about that later." Grandpa Able prodded Jacob almost constantly about everything from his intentions toward Jane to how the football team was shaping up this year. When they had finished eating, Jacob cleared the table and then helped Jane finish the dishes while the two grandparents sat in the living room watching the news.

"Seven confirmed dead from the rogue wave," the newscaster reported, "and in more strange happenings around the city, the Lester River experienced a surge of water today that is thought to be caused by the opening of a previously unknown fresh water spring. City engineers are checking every bridge crossing to make the instant flood didn't damaged the support structures. When the city workers finished checking the river, they said it had returned to its banks, and they could find no reason behind the surge of water."

Jane nearly dropped the soup pan when she heard the report.

"Thankfully, no one was injured, and there seems to be no property damage to speak of." The reporter finished with a picture of the river where Jane and Tasker had ambushed the trackers in the background. The river was as it always had been despite the number of men standing around looking down at the water and taking measurements.

"Jacob," Jane hissed over the sound of the sink facet. She stared at the section of river in disbelief. She knew what Tasker had told her but hadn't really believed it until now. The river had changed in both worlds and then return to normal in both worlds.

"What?" he asked. He dipped the bowls under the water one at a time watching as the soapy residue slid off into the sink.

"I did that," Jane said as she used her towel to point at the television in the living room. Jane explained to him what had taken place while he was sleeping under the fairy spell.

"So, just by drawing on a map, you can change the features of the ground?" Jacob repeated entirely too loudly while they climbed the steps to her room.

"Shh," Jane hissed as her grandfather looked over at them and smiled. "Not so loud."

Thankfully neither of her grandparents rose, and Jane and Jacob managed to get into her room and close the door without any further interruptions. Then Jane could explain. "He told me what we do in one world is mirrored in the other. That's why we needed to be careful. Now I understand. If someone had been standing on the shore when I drew the river wider, they might have been swept all the way downriver."

They were both wearing sturdy jeans and talked about the things they thought would be useful when they returned to the other world. Each carried a small backpack with a few food items and water bottle stuffed in them. Jacob slid his Leatherman onto his belt. He tightened the laces on his sneakers and then looked at her, "I think I'm ready."

"We don't want to take items through the Divide with us we don't need, so we better hide our phones here with the ringers off in case Grandpa comes up here. I'm going to leave my mom a text saying I'll be out of range of the cell towers. That should give us some extra time in case someone comes looking for us." She turned her ringer to silent and slid the phone under her pillow and motioned for Jacob to do the same. "Is the van still out there?"

There was a small window built into the gable of Jane's room and Jacob looked out the corner of it towards where the van had been parked earlier that day.

"Yup, still sitting there," he confirmed. "What do you have in mind?"

"I think a phone call to the police about a strange van moving through the neighborhood looking at houses would be appropriate before we do anything." Jane retrieved her phone from under the pillow and dialed in nine-one-one to the touch pad. When the operator came on, she used her most scared sounding voice to report the strange vehicle and then gave them Jacob's address. They waited for about fifteen minutes, watching the street together out the gable window, before Jacob called out that he could see a police cruiser approaching.

"Well, I thought maybe this area could use one more, strange occurrence before we left." She unrolled the leather and looked at the area she had penned in around the house. With a few strokes of her pen, she widened the map until it encompassed an area around the van as well, and then sat back and considered what was likely to cause the least amount of trouble. Finally, with a chuckle she began to pen in tiny contour lines on the map marking where the land would rise if there had been just the smallest of hills where the van was now parked. She drew in three lines fairly close together and then joined Jacob at the window to watch. There was an imperceptible movement then a cracking sound as the pavement under the vehicle gave way. As the ground rose into the air it picked up the van until the wheels came free of the ground and the vehicle shook wildly for a moment. Suddenly the doors flew open and three black-robed figures leapt from the side doors just as the cruiser turned onto the street.

"This should be fun," Jane said with a giggle. Immediately the light bar on top of the police car came on as the vehicle screeched to a halt about twenty feet from the van. Two officers emerged and both had the weapons pointed at the confused trackers who were all bent over looking under the van at the street. But the small hill Jane had raised under the van had already disappeared leaving behind only a broken section of pavement.

"I wish I could hear their explanation for this," Jacob said with a laugh as he left his post at the window and sat down on the edge of the bed. "Shall we go?"

"Yeah," Jane replied. "I hope they all end up in padded cells at St Peter's." She gathered her map and the last of her things and rolled them tightly so that they would fit inside the pack and then slung it to her shoulder.

N
W ◇ E
S

Moments later they were both standing outside Tasker's home. In the moonlight, Jane could see the cliff side where the door was located.

"What happened?" Tasker asked. He emerged from the hidden door of his underground lair and looked at them curiously. "I felt the ground move for a moment and then return to normal."

"Trackers were watching our house," Jane explained. "I left them to explain to the police why they were there and why the pavement had suddenly buckled under their van." She held up her hands as he rolled his eyes, "I was careful all right. No one saw and it was such a minor change that no one will think anything different of it. Besides it righted itself almost immediately."

"Fine," Tasker muttered. "This way." He led them back into his workshop and sealed the door behind them. "Puck will meet us here in an underground cavern attached to my workshop."

"Happily there is more than one way out of my workshop," Tasker continued, "and there's a likely place for a meeting in a tunnel that attaches to my workshop. Also, there is a mushroom ring close by so Puck can travel more quickly."

"Mushroom ring?"

"Why not," Tasker muttered in annoyance. "It's just as easy to travel through those as any other way. Now if you don't mind keeping silent for a few moments I need to make sure everything's ready."

Neither Jane nor Jacob could think of anything else to say so they just shook their heads and followed Tasker down the steps into his workshop. To Janes surprise, the entire room was empty. Not a sign remained that it had ever been anything but a storage room cut in the ground.

"What happened to all of your stuff?" Jane asked as she slipped into the room and noticed Bella hovering near the far side. All of the books and tools had simply disappeared. Not even a mark remained on the floor where the tables had once stood.

"I'm about to invite one of the most irritating magical mischief makers in the world to my doorstep," Tasker muttered. "I think it's time to find a better place for my store of knowledge." He motioned to the alcove where the small bed had once been. There was now a door in the back of the alcove and it sat open revealing a rough cut tunnel that went deep into the ground.

Tasker led the three of them down into the ground and away from his empty workshop, holding a torch high above his head. At the back of the group Jacob held another torch and kept glancing nervously behind them as the door closed on its own with a hollow thud. There were no stairs really, just a sloping ramp that led down. Finally the tunnel widened out into a cavern of some size with a pool of water at the center. The water spilled over into a small stream and disappeared down a dark hole in the ground that gave no indication of how deep it went. Off to the side near the right-most edge was a circle of mushrooms that seemed to be lit by a light all of its own.

"When will the meeting happen?" Jane asked as she sat down on a small rock jutting out of the cavern floor.

"Soon," Tasker said cryptically. He motioned for Bella and the two humans to come to where he was standing near the far side of the cavern. "Listen to me. Puck is both highly intelligent and sometimes more than a bit malevolent. He'll try to take advantage of everything he can. Do not speak unless I ask you to. Let me do the talking, and let him wonder why you're here. A bit of uncertainty can be very helpful."

Jane nodded as she walked over to where the little man motioned for them to sit and plopped down on another stone that rose above the floor. This time the rock tipped and nearly sent her sprawling across the ground. But Jacob reached out and caught her as she fell.

"Thanks," Jane said as she smiled up at him.

"Any time," Jacob replied with an answering smile. Instead of releasing his grip on her hand he sat down beside her and held on, not wanting to let go.

They didn't have to wait long for the arrival of their mysterious visitor. Without warning there was a flash of light, and the mushroom circle seemed to come alive with a power all its own. A bit of light erupted from the top of each of the tall mushrooms, and they gathered together, whirling about in a circle that, for a moment, lit the entire cavern. Then, standing in the middle of the circle, appeared a creature that seemed to be half human and half furry animal. A purple vest covered his torso while the sleeves appeared to have been torn from a jacket with more muted colors and sewn in place. His legs and waist resembled that of a donkey but was covered in much thicker fur then most animals Jane had seen.

"Ah, Tasker," Puck said with a wide smile that was deceptively charming. "That's what they are calling you now, isn't it?"

"It's my chosen name," Tasker replied with an even stare. His glared at the creature before him with open hostility.

"Such a tone," Puck smiled. "You're still not angry over the whole nibelungen affair are you? I swear to you I didn't take your treasure." Puck looked over at Bella and winked at her with a wide smile.

"Not now, Puck," Tasker muttered as his eyes narrowed. "I didn't call you here to discuss old betrayals. We have a mutual problem to discuss right now."

Puck seemed to consider that a minute. He nodded. His smile faded and a seriousness settled over him.

Tasker didn't like how fast Puck become serious. For the first time he wondered if Cain might be pushing hard on the hobgoblin. It could be that Puck did not have enough of his forces left to even help to them. "Has he attacked you already?" Tasker asked.

"Your former pupil, you mean. Yes, in a way," Puck said in a dangerous tone. He sighed loudly then, and his face stayed serious. "Yes, we do need to talk. Has the NCFC decided to do something about him finally?"

"No, the Northern Committee refuses to do anything from their mountain fortresses," Tasker growled. "And neither will any of the other committees. The Eastern Committee fairly threw me out of the chambers, saying I created the problem and I had to solve it."

"Well, they have a point," Puck replied. "You did give Cain his training . . ." He raised his hands to stop Tasker's angry retort. "I'm not saying there was anything you could have done about his betrayal. All I'm saying is that you *did* train him."

"Yes, I did," Tasker admitted. "Had I known what he would become, I would have turned him away from my door when he approached so many years ago. I've spent the last fifty years regretting opening my door to him."

"So what do you want from me?" Puck said finally. He sat down next to the pool of water and idly examined Jane and Jacob. Then he turned to the fairy. "How are you, Bella? Any news on your family?"

"No," Bella answered sadly. She fluttered over to Jacob and sat down on his shoulder. The mention of her family seemed to have made the little fairy lose whatever bit of excitement filled her. Her face took on a dejected look. She leaned forward with her elbows on her knees and rested her face in her hands.

"We want to free those held at the Prison Islands," Tasker said. "With the help of those held there, we could potentially free Duluth from Cain's grip. You would gain an ally here in the north even if it is only until the Seely Court realizes what's happening and comes against us."

Puck jerked his head to look at Tasker. He stood and slowly walked toward the small man. "You'd go against the orders of the court and recognize my rule? That would go a long way with some of the others. Most of them still respect you. You know that don't you?"

"I realize that," Tasker replied.

"You'd be splitting the Seely Court. It would probably take them hundreds of years to decide what to do. By the time they moved, I could have my minions so entrenched in the woods that nothing could touch us." Puck continued as though no one else was present. "No, no. I need more than that. I need a port on the lakes at the very least. I can't trust the humans or even the frost giants to move my cargo. With my own people moving iron and goods, I can flood the trade ports with cheap iron and rake in a fortune."

"Two Harbor is the only port that will be under our control outside Duluth," Tasker pointed out.

"Why not Duluth itself," Puck said with a sly smile. "I don't want control of the city, just access to the port, and some help learning the craft of ship building."

Tasker sighed. "You do realize that you'll have to cut deals with Mazu, Lir, and Aegir at the very least. The oceans are as filled with boundaries as the land. Maybe more so."

Puck waved his hand dismissively. "I'm on good terms with most of the water creatures. It's the Seely Court that hates me for some reason."

"Probably because you used to draw their young ones away with promises that never seemed to come true." Tasker pointed out to the ruler of the northern goblins. "That's why they drove you to the new world."

"Those self-righteous twits sitting on their thrones on the Greatest of Islands. I really despise them. However, I know you pushed them to do that, Tasker," Puck parried, "after your treasure horde was stolen and you blamed it on me. For once I wasn't responsible for something I'm still being blamed for."

"Whatever," Tasker replied with a fair amount of hostility. "Fine. I'll give you access to the port at Two Harbors and . . ." He lifted his hand to ward off the protests. "And I'll supply you with those who know how to build ships. In return you will help us free those from the Prison Islands and . . ." Again he held up his hand. "And supply Duluth the iron it needs at cost. I need a way to strengthen the defenses here for what will surely someday be war."

Puck leaned back and looked at Tasker with his eyes narrowed. Jane saw the greed erupt, and it shook her just a bit because it looked dangerous. It wasn't just about the money for this creature. It was about the control he craved and the power he wanted. Suddenly the hobgoblin turned his eyes to her and looked at her shrewdly.

"And what of that pair of humans with Bella," Puck asked not willing to agree to the deal quite yet. "What's their part in all of this?"

"She just wants her sister back. She was taken by Cain," Tasker offered. "Will you agree or not?"

"Yes," Puck muttered finally. He waved his hand. With a flourish, a feather-topped pen appeared from inside his coat. He looked around. "Shall we make it official?"

Tasker reached inside his own coat and produced a small piece of parchment that looked almost like a thick sheet of paper. He waved his own hand, and a feather pen appeared out of thin air and began scratching across the surface of the parchment.

Jane leaned forward, wanting to see what was written on the paper, but Bella pulled back on her and shook her head.

"Let them finish," Bella whispered in her ear. This time the fairy settled on Jane's shoulder and leaned forward a little herself, as with a flash of light words began to roll across the surface of the vellum. The words were written in gold in a flowing script that neither Jane nor Bella could make out from where they were sitting.

Puck stopped to peruse the words when they stopped flowing across the document, and when he seemed satisfied he signed it with a flourish. Then he stepped back so Tasker could sign his own name to the bottom of the agreement. With a flash of light, the treaty duplicated itself, and each of them picked up a copy. Puck tucked his away into a pocket in his baggy vest and smiled as he bowed to Tasker.

"It is agreed then," Puck said with a smile. "I will go gather those of my forces who live closest to the Prison Isles. We will meet you at the mushroom circle at Bayfield. From there we can get to the first of the islands fairly quickly. However," Puck muttered, "getting us across to the islands is up to you, Tasker. If you can get my goblins on the shores, we will rescue the prisoners."

"We'll get you across," Tasker said.

"What about the garrison at Madeline Island. They fortified the island with a castle over the last few years," Puck asked. There was a sly smile on his face as he watched Tasker's features darken. "You did know that didn't you? Cain has put much into defending it, almost a thousand troops, half a dozen warships, and now the walls of a castle."

"That I did not know."

"My spies said it appeared almost overnight," Puck continued. "Seemed like magic to them."

"I'll deal with it." Tasker replied with an irritated shake of his head. "Just go gather your goblins and maybe a couple trolls and a giant. I'm sure you have a few favors you can call in to make that happen."

Puck laughed as he walked to the mushroom circle. He was gone with a flash of light.

CHAPTER THIRTEEN
Running the Divide

T IME FOR ANOTHER LESSON, YOU TWO," Tasker said as he tucked the treaty into his vest. Tasker motioned for Jane and Jacob to come closer. "Listen to me, both of you. Cartographers can do amazing things with their maps. but when working with a runner, they can become that much more potent. That, Jacob, is what I believe you are."

"And what exactly is a runner?" Jacob asked.

"Simply put, a skilled runner moves through his cartographer's map and the two worlds almost seamlessly," Tasker said with a gleam in his eye. "A skilled runner can leave waypoints marked on the map that he used for the cartographer to travel also. Most importantly, if we can bring two maps together, the runner can use the other map as well, as long as it is connected to his cartographer's map."

"Wait a minute. You mean if I find a part of one of Cain's maps, we can use it to our advantage?"

"It would be dangerous, but yes," Tasker admitted. "There are some limitations to that from what I've read, but it's possible for a talented runner to travel to a place marked on any map. The reason it's dangerous is that other maps must be accessed from the Divide, and the return to our map must be completed through the Divide."

"But all I saw was a wall of darkness when I passed through," Jane said.

"That's because you're not a runner, my dear," Tasker said to her.

"That's not what I saw," Jacob said. "Well, the first time through I didn't see much of anything, but these last times I saw different things when I entered the wall of darkness. Like floating patches where the darkness was thinner. There were lines and features."

Tasker nodded quickly. "Other maps that are close by," he said. "Don't try and enter them unless you know who the cartographer is who controls them. It's possible that they can see your movements and interfere with you."

"So, you're telling me I can go anywhere and appear anywhere covered by Jane's map?" Jacob said with a gleam in his eyes.

"Before you begin believing in your own tremendous power, understand that some limitations come with the ring," Tasker said as he grabbed Jacob's arm and forced him to look down at him. "Instead of using the anchor which draws its power from the world around us, the ring draws its power directly from the person wearing it." He paused and looked at Jacob. "Do you understand what that means?"

"I'll get more tired each time?" Jacob asked slowly as the light dawned in his eyes.

"Exactly," Tasker replied. "But not just tired. It's possible for you to over-extend your own energy so far that you no longer possess the strength to leave the Divide. In essence you would become lost in the Divide forever. Never try to cross over if you start feeling sleepy and confused. To fall asleep or get lost in the Divide is the same as death."

"But how," Jane started, feeling her way. "If one of our maps is connected to a map Cain controls, then it could be visible to him, and he might be able to see what we're doing as well as where we are. What if he finds out that Jacob is on his map and decides to destroy it?"

Tasker shook his head. "Jacob could be lost forever. As for you, Jane, do not over-extend yourself either. You must never try to destroy things drawn on the map. That tends to cause problems."

"What kind of problems?" Jane asked curiously.

"Girl, the world was created for a reason. The creator isn't going to just let us go around undoing what was put in place," Tasker replied.

"I don't believe that anyone created the world," Jacob said stubbornly.

"Makes no difference whether you believe it or not," Tasker said. "Belief or unbelief doesn't change the truth. Humanity is one of the few races that thinks that if they don't believe in something it doesn't exist. It's really quit silly of you."

Jane opened her mouth to protest but closed it just as quickly. What she had said did sound a bit arrogant, she had to admit. It wasn't that simple, she decided. She still didn't believe that there was anything else out there besides . . . Suddenly her train of thought stopped again. Here she was standing in the middle of a world that mirrored her own and was populated by every legend ever told. Maybe she did need to take a closer look at what she believed.

They sat in silence for a few minutes before Tasker unrolled his map and nodded to Jacob. "I'm going to add your anchor to my map. I want you to try moving about, but not too much. You don't do us any good if you fall over from exhaustion." He leaned over and penned in a small ring in the legend of his map. As they watched, the small ring appeared alongside the marker that placed Tasker himself on the map. "Jacob, the books I've read say the map you're linked to will shine brightest. Don't choose the dark maps, because we do not know who they belong to. If the owner of those maps is watching and sees your anchor appear on his map, he can erase it and leave you stranded. If you enter the Divide without an anchor point, you'll have all the maps in the world to choose from and some can lead to some very dangerous places."

Jacob nodded and looked down at the ornately drawing map of Lake Superior and the surrounding countryside. He studied the map before him for a moment and then narrowed his eyes in concentration and vanished from their sight.

"Now what?" Jane asked as she watched the map.

"We give him a moment to sort it out in the Divide," Tasker muttered. "And we wait for his marker to reappear on my map."

N
W ◇ E
S

THIS TIME, ENTERING THE DIVIDE was easy for Jacob. He seemed to slice through the wall of darkness like a warm knife through butter. Once inside the Divide, he looked about and got his bearings. Just to his right was a wide rectangular map that showed the area around Duluth and covered much of Lake Superior. It took him a moment to sort out where Gooseberry Falls was located, but then he dove headlong into the map and focused his mind on the woods just outside the visitor's center near the falls.

One moment he was standing in the darkness of the Divide, and the next second he was stumbling out of the pine trees and bumping headlong into a hand railing meant to separate tourists from the frothy waters of the Gooseberry River. It was dark out, and the only lights were carrying over from the nearby parking lot and the brilliantly lit visitor's center. Immediately he felt the slight drag at his body, as though he had just run a one-hundred-yard dash and pulled up at the finish line.

"Fascinating," Jacob said as a sense of wonder and excitement left his face warm and his breathing heavily. With a sense of power, he knew he could go anywhere in a moment. In the blinking of an eye, he could move at will. He concentrated on a rocky ledge in the middle of the falls and moments later he was standing atop the rocks looking down at the swirling waters. With a laugh he jumped back to Tasker and Jane. When he arrived he grabbed Jane and swung her around.

"I take it, it went well?" Jane said when he finally released her.

"That was amazing!" Jacob bubbled excitedly. "It's better than the first time I played football." He stopped and caught his breath, "And maybe like the first time I ran two miles." He laughed as he felt his body starting to recover from the strain of running the Divide

"Well, the rest of us will have to travel using the mushroom ring," Tasker said. "I would like to get some rest before Puck has gathered his minions, but I'm hoping to enlist the aid of one more ally. One that Puck doesn't realize is on our side. It will give us the advantage when Puck decides to try and backstab us, and he will."

"Is he really that bad?" Jane asked.

"There's one thing I learned a long time ago. Never trust a hobgoblin unless you have a knife at his throat," Tasker said with a dark look. "The creature I have in mind is very powerful and would make an excellent knife to keep pointed at Puck's throat."

"Are you talking about Yerdarva the red?" Bella asked. She fluttered her wings excitedly.

"Who is Yerdarva," Jane asked curiously.

"Not who," Bella said with a smile. "*What* is Yerdarva? She's one of the few dragons to make the trip to the new world. She's also one of the few dragons still active in the world despite what's considered the legendary horde she's collected."

"She lives in an underground cavern carved into Ringrose Peak above Lake O'Hara in the Mountains of Canada," Tasker said. "Thankfully she created a mushroom ring close by so that those who wished to hire her could reach her more easily."

"Why would she help us?" Jane asked curiously.

"Because Cain has spent years preaching against dealing with dragons. As a result few seek her aid anymore," Tasker explained. "He knows a dragon is a power unto itself, a power that he would be hard pressed to defeat. He most likely would win the battle but it would be at huge loss of power."

"Are you coming with us, Bella?" Jacob asked as they walked to the mushroom ring.

"Yes," Bella responded. "Almost my entire family is being held captive by those allied with Cain. This is my only chance to save them."

"Step inside the ring, and I'll bring us to the right place," Tasker said, motioning to the circle.

"How many of your family has he captured," Jane asked. Thoughts of her sister still floating through her mind and the loss she had felt through the entire ordeal.

"Almost a hundred," Bella small voice said as the lights began to flash around them.

Jane's eyes went wide when the small fairy told her how many of her family was missing. And she'd thought her life had been horrible after Jackie's disappearance. Now she imagined going through that pain and loss a hundred times.

The lights around them flashed faster and faster. Suddenly they were spinning around in circles and sinking down into the ground. When the spinning lights cleared they were traveling at a tremendous speed through the ground in what appeared to be a round tube. Jane felt like she was on a ride at a water park. There were twists and turns and intersections that came and went, and Tasker kept them moving so fast that the moment she saw the turns they went by.

Then in the distance she could see a round circle of light. Moments later they erupted out of the mushroom circle and looked out over the serene waters of Lake O'Hara high in the Canadian mountains. On either side of the trail, pine trees rose, deflecting the chilly air that flowed off the mountains that cut deeply into their clothes. Exiting the ring was an exciting affair as they shot up into the air and then the magic of the mushrooms lowered them slowly to the ground.

"Little cool up here yet," Jacob said as he zipped his light jacket tighter against the wind. The pine trees rustled loudly, and the wind stirred ripples across the surface of the lake and then went on their way again leaving the water calm.

"We need to get around the lake and meet her," Tasker pointed to the right where a massive hole had been bored into the cliff side that came down from the mountain and met the lake. "She makes people walk to her so she can examine them as they approach and decide if they are honest traders or thieves coming to try and steal from her."

"What would anyone trade with a dragon for?" Jacob asked suddenly. He turned it around in his mind as he pondered what a dragon would have to offer.

"Dragon's fire, boy," Tasker muttered. "Best thing in the world to refine iron, gold, silver, and pretty much anything else that can be refined. One blast of dragon's fire leaves only the purest of metals and completely burns off everything else."

They hiked around the lake towards the dark cavern as fast as the light of the moon would let them, and the silvery orb was high overhead when they finally arrived before her lair. Jane started forward but Tasker put out his hand to stop her as Bella grabbed her jacket and pulled.

"Never enter a dragon's lair uninvited," Bella explained as Tasker took a step closer and waited. "That's a good way to find out how hot dragon's fire truly is."

"Wise advice, Bella," a voice spoke from the darkness.

Jane found the voice to be cultured and polite but it spoke with a slightly serpentine quality. She looked into the darkness eagerly hoping to catch a glimpse of the creature who spoke. Then she heard the scraping of a massive body moving in the darkness and the sound of scales rubbing against rocks as the dragon emerged into the night air.

"Why have you come here, Tasker?" Yerdarva asked.

"We need help," Tasker said as he looked up at her.

Jane examined the dragon and found that she was a thing of beauty, a long scaly neck led to a head that was as large as a Volkswagen. Her body was almost the size of a dump truck and each of her legs ended in a set of claws that easily scored the stones under her movements. Her eyes in particular caught Jane's attention—great pools of liquid gold that spoke of great intelligence and even greater age.

"Is it Cain," Yerdarva asked. She spit out the words with such venom that it surprised all of them.

"Yes," Tasker admitted. "My former pupil has gone beyond what any of us thought he would. We surrendered territory to him in hopes of appeasing him, but it didn't last. The rest of the committees refuse to interfere, and it'll be to their deaths. If we don't take a stand now, he'll take control of the entire continent."

"I thought so," Yerdarva said. "You see I received another visitor this morning, one who, like you, did not come offering trade. Instead he came with a warning for me."

"Cain came here?"Tasker said as his eyebrows shot up and he looked around quickly. "And you didn't kill him?"

"He did not stay," Yerdarva said. "He left a few of his watchers, but I found them quickly and burned them out in my rage. Sadly I can't help you."

Jane glanced around at the surrounding mountains and suddenly realized that in the distance fires were burning on many of the slopes. Great swathes of destruction cut by the creature before them.

"Why?" Tasker asked, stunned. He looked up at the magnificent dragon and wondered what his former pupil could have done to keep the noble dragon from interfering in something that was bound to make her horde swell much more quickly.

"This morning was not the first time he's visited my cavern,"Yerdarva admitted. "But the last time I was not here and he took something very dear to me. If I come to your aid, he will destroy what he has taken."

"Your offspring?"Tasker asked quietly.

"I was hunting elk that morning, and I felt the magical barriers I placed around the cavern break. I came back as quickly as I could,"Yerdarva explained. "It took me mere moments to return from the mountains, but he had time to take one thing—my only egg was gone. He came back today to tell me that if I interfered with his plans in any way he could destroy the egg and send my child back to me in pieces."

Tasker shook his head and grumbled under his breath.

"I won't go with you," Yerdarva said. "I can, however, give a small bit of aid. Come into my lair out of the weather and we will speak of it. I don't think I missed any of his watchers but better to be safe."

They followed her into the cavern, and Jane was amazing that the chill wind from outside failed to penetrate even an inch into the cavern. The moment they entered the lair, the air became warm and moist. Jane removed her outer jacket immediately. The cavern extended down at a slight angle into the heart of the mountain, they walked for about three hundred yards through a cave that seemed to have been torn by sharp claws from the bedrock of the mountain. When they reached the interior of the lair, the tunnel opened up in a wide cavern whose ceiling soared up in a natural formation to five times the height of the outer tunnel. In the exact center of the lair was a mound of shimmering treasure that left Jane's mouth dry. Piles of gold coins and loose gemstones lay in the center while items of various sizes were scattered all over the mound of treasure. Greedy thoughts suddenly filled her, and her hands twitched nervously in her pockets.

"Your hoard has grown some since the last time I was here," Tasker said as he looked at the mound. There was a glint in his eyes as he looked out across the mounds of treasure. He slowly licked his lips.

"Don't get greedy," Yerdarva said with a silky smile. "There is only room for one greedy creature in this cavern."

They both laughed as she slithered towards the hoard and began daintily sorting through it and laying things off to the side. "I'm going to give you some things to help even the odds with the Adherents. Call it a long-term loan that I'll expect repaid some day."

"Any help you can give us would be much appreciated," Tasker replied. He tore his gaze away from the mounds of treasure and smiled ruefully at Bella. "I guess I should have worried more about bringing myself here than the others. There was a day when my own treasure vault was equal to this."

"For the boy who I assume is a runner by the looks of the ring on his hand and the anchor on his chest," Yerdarva said, "this shield will defend him from magic and the blade. It's made from one of my own scales and is so strong that the arm holding it will break before it does. Also, since a shield does little good without a weapon," she rummaged for a moment and then produced a sword inside a silver scabbard. "This is the sword Frofyre forged at the same time, and the renowned blade Dyrnwyn spoke of in the legends. Its blade will never break, and it will bring its vast knowledge of swordplay to whoever wields it." She laid the two items at Jacob's feet and motioned for him to try the shield and sword.

Jacob leaned over and picked up the shield which was round and red much like Yerdarva's scales yet it was as light as a feather. He worked the straps awkwardly at first until Bella fluttered over and helped him connect them properly. Then he set the sword belt in place around his waist and drew the blade carefully. It gleamed darkly in the bonfires that warmed the cavern and seemed to pull in what light was closest to it.

"Cut one of the rocks with it," Yerdarva instructed. "Test its blade."

Jacob turned and walked to the wall, he swung the blade hesitantly against the stones of the cavern wall not wanting to hurt the blade. It tapped against the wall, weakly leaving a small scratch but didn't harm the blade.

"I said *swing* it against the wall," the dragon roared. Her voice echoed off the mountain side and shook bits of dirt free from the ceiling. The massive head and impressive teeth shot forward towards Jacob as her eyes glittered in the light.

Jacob jumped. This time he swung with all his might and was amazed to see the blade penetrate deeply into the granite of the mountain and yet pull free just as easily.

"And you, young cartographer," Yerdarva said as she turned back from Jacob. "Because I feel that is who you are, this map case is for you. If you place any maps inside, it will protect them from being used by anyone else. They will not even appear to runners moving through the Divide."

The case she handed Jane was nearly the size of her arm and round, with a leather strap that could be slipped around her head and shoulder for ease in carrying it. The case was bound with seven gold straps. A spider web of smaller gold strings filled in the areas between the straps. "The gold is enchanted and will keep the case safe from harm. Taking someone's maps from him one at a time and binding them inside the case, is to take his power from him." The dragon's voice hissed in barely contained rage.

"Do I get something too," Bella said excitedly. Her wings buzzed nearly as fast as a hummingbird as she fluttered closer to the dragon and looked about with wide eyes.

"Many of the items I've collect over the centuries are much too large for your arms to hold, fairy," Yerdarva said sadly. Then she smiled widely and turned back to her great hoard, "However, there's one thing you may find useful. It was made with magic for a young boy that has long since passed from this world." She turned and walked to the hoard of treasure and finally returned with a small silver case. The dragon opened it and removed a delicate bow and quiver of arrows from inside. It was the perfect size for Bella to wield.

Tears streamed down the little fairy's face as she carefully fitted the quiver between her wings and took the tiny bow from between Yerdarva's claws.

"It's called the half-moon bow. The arrows are small, but the quiver will refill itself when the moon peaks each night," the dragon explained. "There are fifty arrows in the quiver. Use them well. With a bit of luck, you won't run out before midnight each day."

Bella nodded. She wrapped her tiny arms as far around the dragon's neck as they would go and gave her a great hug. "With this I'll free my family." Bella said happily. She fluttered back to sit on Janes shoulder.

"To you, Tasker, I give you only this, my promise," Yerdarva said as she rose to her full height. "If you can return my egg to me, I'll join you in your cause and rain fire and destruction on Cain's forces wherever I can find them. That's my promise to you until my strength fails and I must return to my lair to rest." Her voice grew dark and bits of fire erupted from around her mouth as she spoke.

Jane shrank back from the massive serpentine body as fear coursed through her veins. She could see why most would avoid the great creatures. Power filled the scaled body, a power that could hollow a mountain out and destroy entire forests.

"You've given us great help, noble dragon," Tasker said. "I only hope we can achieve our goals."

Yerdarva escorted them back to the mushroom ring. As they stepped inside and began to spin around and around, she spoke one last time. "This is the last time this mushroom ring will be used until Cain's power is broken. Be warned that any attempt to come through it will be met with dragon's fire, unless you come with my egg, and that I will know before you arrive."

Tasker nodded and then they were gone.

CHAPTER FOURTEEN
Puck's Goblins

THE PASSAGE UNDER THE MUSHROOM circle flashed by. Suddenly Jane found herself standing with the others in the middle of a dense forest. She heard a rustling in the trees around her and could vaguely see the shadows of creatures moving about in the underbrush. Suddenly the grinning face of Puck erupted before them and nodded to Tasker.

"I found who I could on short notice," Puck said. "It was not easy though. Cain's soldiers have been pushing my followers hard in the past weeks. We lack the strength to fight back in any way more serious then harassing their flanks."

"How many did you bring?" Tasker asked.

"There will be three hundred here by sunset tonight that I can count on in a fight," Puck replied. He held up his hands as Tasker snorted at the small number. "I count two giants and a trio of trolls among that group. As long as we take the islands one at a time and can avoid any major battles, we should be fine."

"Three hundred and three against a thousand trained soldiers," Tasker muttered. "Yes, it should be a walk in the meadows." He rubbed his face and squinted to where the sun was beginning to rise in the east out across the lake. "We need to stay under cover of the forest until this evening when all the ships are docked and all the slaves are back in their holding areas." Tasker looked pointedly at Puck. "You must control your groups here already until this evening. These two and I have some scouting to do."

Tasker and Puck walked away for about ten minutes to strategize. While Jane and Jacob waited, they talked privately for some time. When Tasker and Puck returned, Tasker seemed to be satisfied with what Puck had told him and motioned to Jane. "Be ready when the signal is given."

"We'll be ready to do our part this evening," Puck repeated. "Just be sure to provide us a way across the water." The hobgoblin turned away and motioned several of his followers over to where he was standing.

Tasker waved his hand to the hobgoblin, and then led Jane and Jacob away from the mushroom ring and into the thick forest that bordered the lake where the town of Bayfield, Wisconsin, would have been in their world. There was an abundance of apple trees filling dozens of meadows, but this early in the summer the fruit was still the size of cherries. No town existed in this world, but there were signs that attempts had been made to establish a village, though it had been abandoned and weeds were overtaking the ruins of the cottages.

"I can't believe there are so many beautiful apple trees and no village," Jacob said.

"Oh, and the apples are the juiciest, most delicious practically anywhere," Tasker said as he led them north along the shore. "People come from miles around for them. The Bayfield pixies have always done great work preparing the apple harvest. It's what keeps Cain from driving them away."

Jane wanted to argue that pixies didn't exist when suddenly she noticed a tiny face staring down at her from high in an apple tree and she clamped her mouth shut. The pixie was small, only half the size of Bella who was fluttering nearby with her bow ready, and a tiny pair of antennae stuck up from the top of her head. Jane smiled hesitantly as the tiny creature smiled and waved at her. She waved back slowly and then the tiny creature was gone almost as quickly as it had appeared. From now on Jane resolved, *I won't to challenge the existence of anything in this world.*

They walked through the orchards. The land around them was rolling hills. Stretches of forest separated the orchards, and dozens of narrow trails cut through the brush in the stretches of trees and warned of almost constant use by the Adherents.

"Where are we going?" Jane asked finally when Tasker motioned for them to stop. He was standing near a stone outcropping peering down at the rocky cliffs that dropped down to meet the lake.

"To find ourselves a ship or two," Tasker said. "We need something to move our forces out to Sand Island. We are going to take that island first because I think it's the least guarded and is the furthest from Madeline Island, which we know is heavily guarded." He motioned for them to join him and then pointed down past the rocky outcropping.

Jane looked down at the lakeshore in front of her. Sticking out from a section of beach were three wooden piers with their cross beams set into the tops of great stone pillars that pushed their heads out of the water almost ten feet. At each of the piers were two ships, disgorging long lines of slaves that tramped down the docks and disappeared into a tunnel carved into the rocky cliff. Tasker whispered to them that, later in the year the slave masters would be ordering their charges out into the orchards to tend the groves and pick those apples that the pixies had ripened over the summer.

The ships themselves were small cargo carriers with ten banks of oars built into their sides and a cargo hold where the mined ore would be taken and, in the fall, baskets of apples would be stowed.

"This is where we will start," Tasker muttered quietly. He turned back and leaned down behind the boulder that sheltered them. "We'll return here before dark. Teams of slaves have probably been sent up to the many meadows to pick strawberries. Those working in the closer meadows always return first, and they always leave before those assigned to the outer meadows. We'll wait until the last two ships are all that are left. Then we'll make our move. Once we have those two ships, we'll take Sand Island and then move east. Each slave we free who can fight will bolster our numbers."

Jacob nodded, "What do we do until then?"

"We," Tasker said, "and by that I mean you and Jane must build an accurate map of the islands so you can be our ace, moving quickly between the islands and reassuring the slaves still held that we're coming. And you'll need to calm them before the goblins begin moving. There will be a fair amount of distrust to overcome between the slaves and Puck's forces. Thankfully both sides hate the Adherents more than each other."

"How do we make such a huge map?" Jane asked as she knelt down beside Tasker.

"Mostly you'll copy a section of mine," Tasker said as he indicated a section of his map. As she began hurriedly sketching that area of his map, Tasker continued, "The other thing we need to know is how many are being held on Madeline Island and who's there."

Jane's hand faltered for a moment but then she continued as she forced the image of her sister from her mind. Now was the time to focus on the task at hand.

"Jacob," Tasker motioned him over. "You need to visit each island as it shows up on her map. Try to make contact and reassure the prisoners that they are not forgotten. More importantly, find out how many guards are on each island and verify how many are on Madeline Island. Above all do not over-extend yourself. You'll do us little good if you spend the rest of your life wandering the Divide in darkness forever."

It took Jane nearly an hour to finish sketching in the main outer islands marked on Tasker's map. She made sure to place boundaries on her own map, not wanting to come in contact accidently with a map that was much bigger than her own. "I think you can start, Jacob," Jane said as she looked up. "I'll continue with the bigger islands while you check out the smaller ones."

Jacob nodded as he nervously twisted the ring on his hand, "Add me to your map, and I'll see what I can see." He made sure the straps on his new shield were held tightly in place and then tightened the belt holding his sword in place by a notch. Right now he was filled with nervous energy and he had the feeling he would need every ounce of it before this day was done.

JACOB SLIPPED INTO THE DARKNESS of the Divide now easily and he was amazed at how fast moving between the worlds and the Divide had become. There floating nearby was Jane's map, and he watched as she continued to draw and more outlines of islands appeared before him. He could see another map floating nearby, but all it contained was an outline of a castle atop Madeline Island. The lake shore was marked for a distance and then the far side of the map stretched out to the northeast beyond his ability to see.

He looked at the map curiously for a few moments and then slipped into Jane's map and stepped out onto one of the smaller islands. He tried to remember the map he and his mom had bought when they visited the islands last year and he thought the one he was about visit was called Sand Island. There was a gasp as he appeared, and he looked around quickly, hoping not too many people had seen his arrival.

"Who are you?"

Jacob turned to face the speaker and found himself face to face with the willowy figure with slightly pointed ears looking at him curiously. He crouched instinctively. All around him were crude huts built of drift wood and thatched with straw that looked to be too old to keep out any water. He had seen pictures of thatching in a history book, and it was similar to what the slaves had attempted. Without the constant repair that thatching required he doubted these roofs would keep anything dry.

"Who are you?" she asked again. The woman was dressed in the remains of a tattered gown and a cloak made of what appeared to be coarse burlap. It hung off her thin frame in a shapeless gathering of material.

"My name is Jacob," he answered when it appeared no one in a black robe was near. "Please tell me—are there any guards nearby?"

"No, they all leave with the ship in the morning," she answered. "My name is Patalia."

"Nice to meet you," Jacob said. His eyes widened slightly when he really looked around the island. The slaves lived in horrible conditions. A pair of watch towers rose in the distance, but they looked to be empty. All around him the crude huts huddled together as though those living in them were trying to keep out the cold with just their closeness.

"Is it like this everywhere?" Jacob asked as he slowly rose to his feet. He could see two or three young children with great big eyes and pointed ears looking at him from the darkened doors of the huts. There was no animosity that he could see, just curiosity and resigned hopelessness. On each of those visible, a yellow letter was emblazoned on whatever they wore, and it sometimes seemed that it was the only thing they had that looked new.

"Some of the islands near Madeline Island are better, but they are also closer to the Adherents," Patalia said. She pointed to the south and then continued. "I would rather live out here then be too close to those foul creatures."

Jacob held up his hands. "I don't have a lot of time," but then he saw the pretty being cringe and draw away from him. He shook his head. "Please I mean you no harm, but I must know if there are any on this island who would be able to fight if the chance was offered."

Suddenly there was a flash in the elf's eyes, and she stood proudly, "All of us would if we thought there was a chance of escape. But it's no use. We're kept in these conditions for a reason. What little magic we still can use is put to keeping us alive. There is none left over for anything that could be turned against the soldiers and their abomination weapons. Those foul creations are beyond our ability to fight." The resignation appeared in her eyes again and sadness filled them, "We are a lost people just waiting to be worked to death."

"How many guards are here at night?"

"About a score at each side of the island. They stay near the watch towers and close to the ships, but they're well-armed with swords and those muskets the Adherents use."

"Jacob's blank look must have told her that he didn't understand because she explained further. "About twenty on each side."

"All right," Jacob said. "Please tell those who come back that help is coming. You are not forgotten." Hope seemed to stir in Patalia, and it erupted in her eyes. She grabbed him and wrapped him a great hug. Tears rolled down her face as she stepped back and nodded.

"I'll tell those we trust," Patalia replied. "And we know those who spy for the Adherents, they will be dealt with before you come."

Jacob stepped back into the Divide and examined the map Jane was drawing. Another tiny island lay just to the west, but he decided to save that one for later. Instead he went to the east and entered the one be remembered as Bear Island. He and his mother had visited Bayfield several times over the years and he knew the area fairly well.

His arrival this time seemed to have gone unnoticed and he slipped behind one of the few trees. From his vantage point he could see a single tower rising above the island and a fenced compound surrounding it. Many of the trees on this side of the Divide had been stripped from the island and the few stands that remained separated huts built of stone and topped with old thatch. Few people moved about, but everyone Jacob could see seemed to be human, and all of them were bound with chains. Suddenly his heart leapt into his throat as he heard a shuffling of footsteps behind him and heard a rumbling grunt from something nearby. He turned his head slowly. Seated on the ground behind him was a wolf-like creature immense in size. Its head was nearly the size as a horse's and its fangs were long and sharp as daggers.

The creature pulled back its lips and smiled at him then it spoke. "I thought I smelled something close by."

Jacob gasped as the creature looked him up and down. Then leaned over to sniff at him. Its eyes were tinged with red and he narrowed them at Jacob. "Why are you here?" the wolf asked. "You smell like one from the other side. My employer would not like finding you here."

"I . . . um . . ." Jacob faltered as his hand inched nervously towards his sword.

"I wouldn't do that if I were you," the wolf growled, and the hair on the back his great neck rose and his eyes narrowed into vicious red slits. "I can gut you before you even get close to drawing it. On the other paw, it may be you can put up your shield and stop my fangs long enough for you to draw your blade. Dragon-scale shields are not common, and I don't know how my teeth will fare against it. So we're back to my original question. Why are you here?"

"You must know that what Cain is doing here is wrong," Jacob blurted out finally. His hands were shaking. He found is terrifying to be addressing the monstrous wolf, but he had little choice but to make his case.

"Wrong by whose standards?" the wolf countered with a slight smile.

"By any decent per . . . being's," Jacob said, not wanting to prejudice his case by insulting a creature clearly not a "person" in his understanding.

The wolf must have decided that he was not a threat because it sat back on its haunches and watched him closely. "The strong always prey on the weak," the wolf replied. "Why should I care who I work for? I am, after all, one of the strongest of . . . beings, and I'm paid well to keep the inhabitants of Bear Island under control at all times."

"But these people are slaves," Jacob said as he finally found the courage to rise to his feet. "How can you be a part of keeping these poor souls in slavery?"

"Have you seen the worst inhabitants of Bear Island? Those wearing the chains here in the inner villages are the least of your worries," the wolf said as it cocked its head to the side. "Come, we'll go see those evil creatures that still remain here, those too wild and violent to work. Worry not, young one, the Adherents are gone. All that remains on this island are those deemed too savage to work."

Jacob looked about fearfully but finally rose and followed the wolf out into the open areas. As he jogged along behind the wolf, he began to realize that the island was covered in more than stone huts. He also saw dozens of wide holes carved into the ground. Near one of these holes they stopped.

"Look down at the poor slaves you came to worry about and tell me if you think we do the world an injustice by keeping them here." The wolf sat back on its haunches and nodded for Jacob to look over the edge.

Jacob pulled his eyes away from the massive creature and edged closer to the lip of the hole and looked down, suddenly there a snarl of rage and something tried to scramble up the wall. A wicked-looking set of claws reached towards him. He fell backwards and his heart raced. He finally managed to pull his sword from its scabbard and point it at the hole.

"It can't get out. It's chained to the stones at the bottom of the pit," the wolf said to him in amusement. "And you should be happy that it can't. It killed nearly a score of the Adherents before they finally managed to contain it, and it would continue killing until it was killed itself if freed."

"What is it?" Jacob gasped as he edged closer and looked down again. The monster at the bottom of the pit was similar to a bear in appearance but much leaner, and its eyes glowed red with an almost inner light.

"The native people who once lived in these woods before your people drove them out called them wendigo. Some believed it was the spirit of a lost hunter who died on the hunt and his soul refused to give up that same hunt. There are few left and for the most part they live in the forests and keep to themselves. Of course when my master began cutting down the forests, he disturbed this one and it was sent here."

"I—" Jacob began

The wolf cut him off. "So where shall we begin freeing the poor creatures held captive on this island?" the wolf asked with a sadistic grin. "Here or somewhere else?"

"Tasker never mentioned these kind of monsters being held captive," Jacob muttered.

"Tasker?" the wolf said suddenly. The wolf sat up a bit straighter and looked at him with a gleam in his eyes.

Inwardly Jacob kicked himself for mentioning the little man's name to the giant wolf.

"Is that who sent you?" the wolf asked. "Did he tell you what happened the last time he tried to free the slaves here?"

"He . . . what do you mean 'last time'?" Jacob asked suddenly as his blood ran cold. Tasker had tried this before and failed. The news was like a bucket of cold water being dumped over his head. A chill ran down his spine and he waited for the wolf to continue. Why hadn't the little man mentioned this last attempt? Had it been that bad of a disaster?

"This is not the first time he's tried to stop Cain," the wolf growled. "Last time the pair of humans who came with him both vanished without a trace."

"I didn't know . . ." Jacob muttered and then fell silent.

"The runner he sent last time ended up facing Cain and dying a very painful death," the wolf said with a snort. "And from what I see you're no better than he was. Go back to your little friend and tell him to give up. We can't stop Cain. The sooner Tasker accepts that, the sooner people will stop dying." This time the wolf's voice seemed tired and worn, "Go back to him and tell him I won't betray what he plans but neither will I support him or allow anyone who sets foot on this island to live. Bear Island is off limits unless he proves to me this time is different."

Jacob nodded and turned away from the wolf. His mind swirled around and around. Tasker had tried this before and had even recruited a map maker and a runner to help and neither had survived. What would he tell Jane? What would he do? Could he even trust the short dwarf to keep his word, or was he willing to throw their lives away in a desperate attempt to stop someone who they couldn't stop.

The wolf just looked at him and finally shook his mighty head, "Hope is lost, son. Soon you will know why."

Jacob took one last look at the mighty wolf as he faded into the Divide. Then the surface of Bear Island was gone, and he looked at the map once again. This time he choose one that was almost the opposite of Bear Island. As he moved to it, he wondered what he was about to meet. With a snap the surface of Cat Island popped into view, and Jacob wondered if he had made a horrible mistake. Dozens of eyes turned and looked at him, and a score of voices cried out in fear. All around him were creatures drawn straight out of a myriad of legends from around the world. There were great black cats with white spots on their chests, there were small cats that resembled ones he had seen when reading a book about Egypt, even a woman with the head of a cat looking over at him with curiosity.

Immediately a clamor of voice arose and the beings crowded around him, shouting their questions. This time his breath came in short gasps, and he raised his hands to ward off the rush of questions directed towards him, and his energy ebbed and flowed from him. The use of the ring was taking its toll on him. Soon he would need to rest and find something to eat.

"Who are you?"

"Why are you here?"

"Help us please?"

Voices erupted from all around him, and Jacob edged back as he looked about with wide eyes, "Please stop shouting!" he cried finally.

Slowly silence descended on the group, and then one cat being approached him. "Why are you here?" she asked. She scratched idly at the yellow letter sewn into her robe and glared down at it as though it offender her by its mere presence.

"Please, I was sent to speak to the people and creatures," he included hastily, "being held captive on these islands. We are trying to gather support to free everyone." Immediately there was a gasp as a dozen voices once again began to clamor for his attention. The nearest cat hissed them to quiet.

"I'm called Bastet. My ancestors ruled over ancient Egypt before the Divide was put in place. We came here to start over, and this is what we gained—banishment to a tiny island and a group of Adherents to watch over us and keep us in line. They keep us isolated here because we can escape too quickly on the mainland. We'll join you in a moment if you can provide us with a way past the guards. I speak for all those present." Bastet said fiercely. She held up her hand and showed him a formidable set of claws that flexed out almost an inch past the end of her fingers. "Given the chance, my people will bathe their claws in Adherent blood."

"Be ready then because we'll return tonight," Jacob replied. He looked about again trying to count the number of feline creatures present but they moved about so much a true count was impossible. Bastet was clothed in a long robe and a pair of golden sandals protected her feet, but it was her eyes that drew his gaze. Full of pride and hatred when they looked over to where the Adherent guard post sat on the far side of the island.

"They keep watch from there at night and protect the ship that sits just off shore. They know that my people are loath to enter the water and that swimming and sailing are beyond most of our abilities so they are slack in their duties most nights. By midnight those on shore will be drunk and those aboard the ship will be asleep. Take them then and come for us. We will be the sharp claws that take the Adherents from the dark and we can be your eyes and nose to scout where they are weakest."

"I'll be back," Jacob promised as he faded from view again. It was well past midday and Jacob knew he was running low on time. Besides he still had to speak to Tasker about what the wolf had told him. With this in mind, he entered the map where the lake met the main land and scrambled under cover near Jane and Tasker.

CHAPTER FIFTEEN
A White Lie?

B ACK SO SOON?" JANE SAID as she hunched over her map, sketching furiously. Tasker was standing over her pointing to various spots that he thought needed to be marked off better. She glanced up and started to look back at her map but was drawn back to the storm clouds brewing on Jacob's face.

"What happened before, Tasker?" Jacob asked quietly. Suddenly Jane's pen came to a halt, and she looked up. Jacob had slumped to the ground and his head hung wearily as he looked around at the dwarf. He was tired now and needed sleep and food.

"What do you mean before?" Jane asked curiously.

But what attention Jacob could muster was focused entirely on Tasker. "I ran into a wolf the size of a horse," Jacob explained. "He didn't give his name but he was guarding a creature he called a wendigo and who knows what else by the look of that island. There were enough craters in the ground for there to be a dozen of those things back there. He said you tried this before and failed, and the boy and girl that came with you before died horrible deaths at Cain's hands."

Tasker frowned deeply and sat down slowly on a nearby rock as Jane and Jacob looked at him and waited for an answer. "It was different then," Tasker muttered. "They were not the true cartographer and runner. You two are."

"How is it different now?" Jacob insisted. "We can't be captured and held here the rest of our lives. It would kill our parents. What happens if we fail, Tasker? What happens to us? If we die here what happens?"

"Then you die. If we fail and are captured, Cain would probably have you locked away in a place where no map reaches. There are many such places. He has prepared them on the off chance that he finally catches up with me," Tasker admitted. "I have hidden from him for many years while trying to find a way to stop him. Please, you must believe me that this time it is different. You two are different. You are the ones who can defeat him. There's something special about you both." He rubbed his face with his hand as he tried to explain. "Yes, I thought I had found a true cartographer before, but that was nearly thirty years ago, and there was no runner. We tried to stop Cain then, and we failed. I barely escaped with my life. That's what's different. To find you both so close to one another is a gift from he who created the world. He is offering us a chance to defeat a creature of evil, and we have to take it."

Jacob peeked around the corner of the stone and noticed that the first of the ships was pulling away from the pier, and the second seemed to be preparing to leave. They had little time left to decide what to do. He turned to Jane. "What do you want to do?"

"I don't know why you lied to us, Tasker" Jane muttered. She stared at him accusingly, hating the thought that he had lied to her even if it had only been by not telling her the whole truth. A lie was a lie, and it shattered her faith in the little man. Still her sister . . . then she stopped. "Did you lie to me about my sister just to get me to come here and help you?"

"No, I swear to you," Tasker said pleadingly. He was near tears as he watched the second ship slip away from its pier. "She was taken by Cain. I know that and I know he wouldn't kill her." This was the chance, the best chance he had ever had to free the slaves here on the Prison Islands and it was slowly starting to slip away. "Look I believe in both of you. You have shown extraordinary talent. I believe with all my heart that we can free those held here and strike a blow against Cain and his Adherents. It's not just the lands around here that are at risk. Cain's power extends to the great ice flows in the north and east to the Appalachian Mountains and west to the great plains. His territory expands every year because no one will face him. Someone has to step up and make a stand against his sort of evil. Someone has to lead and show those who think they're too weak to stand against him. We have to show the old world that there's strength in the new world. Maybe then they'll see the error of allowing a creature like Cain to run free."

"I have to know if my sister is alive," Jane said finally to Jacob. "But I won't judge you if you want to leave." She said the words slowly, hoping he would stay. The look on his face told a different story, and she knew he wouldn't. He glared angrily at Tasker, and his jaw was set in a firm line.

Jacob rubbed his face with his hands in a gesture that mirrored Tasker's from just a moment ago, "I'm sorry. I can't trust him. I'm going back to our world. I spoke with the people on three islands. I think you should start with Sand Island first and then go to Cat Island. The slaves on those islands are ready and willing to fight if you can get them to a place where they can fight and supply them with some weapons. Whatever you do, don't land on Bear Island. There's a wolf there the size of a horse who said if you land there he'll fight you to the death."

"That's a great help," Jane muttered as she glared at him. Despite her words about not judging, it felt like he was abandoning her. "Thanks for staying this long."

"I'm sorry," Jacob said again. Then he disappeared into the Divide, and a moment later was gone off her map. He knew the words were empty but he couldn't stay.

Jane looked at Tasker and felt alone for the first time since coming here with the little man. Doubts about him despite his assurances still plagued her and would, she knew, for a long time. She knew she had to put those doubts aside for her sister. Her sister was all that mattered. If she could only find her.

Once she and Jackie were back together, she would take her sister and disappear back to their world, that she promised herself.

"Well, your map is ready," Tasker said as he leaned down and looked over the detailed drawing that included all of the Apostle Islands and much of the coast line from Houghten Point all the way north to Sandy Point. He knew it was perfect because he had spent almost a year perfecting his own map of the region, and it matched his perfectly. He had done it without the modern technology available in Jane's world. He had hiked the shore lines and looked down from every hill and measured every stretch of beach until it was perfect. "There still remain a few things yet to learn." He turned around and looked down at the piers where the third ship was now loaded and pulling away into the rougher waters of the lake.

"What's that?" Jane asked curiously. Any bit of information now was being channeled into one purpose, the rescue of her sister.

"A true cartographer can make a change on a map that only affects one side of the Divide," Tasker said. "But the change must be made from inside the Divide." He looked at her, "This is something I was never able to do, and when I tried, the Divide threw me physically back into the world and destroyed the map I was working with. I spent years reconstructing my map."

"So if I fail, I get spit out like a wad of old chewing gum with nothing to show for the effort?" Jane asked with a shake of her head. "This just gets better and better. I thought you said the one who created the world would not let us make anything permanent?"

"It wouldn't be permanent. In fact it would only last a short time, but it can be a huge advantage when we move against the Adherents."

"And we need to move now," Jane said as she looked down towards the piers. The forth ship was being loaded and was almost ready to set out from its pier.

"Listen to me, Jane," Tasker begged. "I'm going to go make sure Puck is in place. He should be ready by now. I need you to enter the Divide and get ready to close off the passage leading to the ships. From there we can rid ourselves of the Adherents guarding the last two groups and get ready to take the ships."

"How will I know?" Jane asked as she rolled up her map and put away her pen.

"I think it'll be completely apparent to you when the time comes," Tasker said with a smile. He nodded to her, "Trust me, Jane. I'm not lying to you. I'm sorry I never told you about the others, but I truly believe that you are the one and that we can do this even without Jacob at our side."

She looked at him and sighed. Inwardly she prayed that her sister was still alive and that they would be together at the end of all this. Even more, she promised herself that if she found her sister she would flee this place and never return. "All right, I'm going in," she muttered. She touched medallion and suddenly the great black wall of the Divide stood before her, this time she stopped herself before she entered it and examined it closely. At first there was nothing. It was simply an empty wall of darkness.

"Wait a minute. What's that?" Jane asked suddenly. Her voice fell in the dead silence around her, but she ignored the sound and looked more closely at the Divide. Now she could see it. The map she had just drawn hovered in front of her on the flat black surface of the Divide. "Still, this doesn't solve my problem," Jane muttered to herself. "I can't see when to do anything." She edged closer to the map and pulled her pen from her pocket. Then it struck her. She needed to see things in three dimensions to close off the tunnel. Carefully she edged even closer until her nose was only a fraction of an inch from the map and examined it. Then she felt the urge to try and enter her own map while it floated in the Divide, and she knew this was what Tasker was talking about. She moved forward until her face was half inside the wall of the Divide and fully contained into her map. Suddenly she found she could see every hill, every tree of the world outside the Divide. Even more, she could move her arms across the surface.

"Amazing," Jane muttered to herself in the darkness. She could see Puck's goblins forming a skirmish line across the edges of the furthest orchard and begin to push into the trees. Here and there she spotted the Adherents guarding the slaves and she watched as the slaves began hauling their loads of strawberries away towards the waiting ships. As she watched, she realized that Puck's goblins would never reach the last group in time, so she reached out with her pen and wiped away the tunnel leading to the ships in broad strokes. With that done, she watched with amusement as the Adherents were suddenly confronted with a wall of stone.

With her task done Jane stepped back into the world and blinked suddenly as the sun once again filled her vision. She emerged at the same overlook and quickly gathered the few things she still had lying on the ground. There were startled shouts coming from the west, and she made her way through the trees towards where the sounds were echoing from.

"What do you mean the tunnel's gone?" a voice shouted. There was a sound of someone grunting as a striking sound echoed across the orchard.

Jane smiled as she hid behind a thick tree and glanced out to where nearly fifty slaves were waiting with their loads of fruit. Above her a small pixie popped its head out of the leafy boughs and looked at her with a smile and a wiggle of its antennae. The pixie smiled and nodded to the small green apple that hung from a branch near Jane's head, she reached out and touched the apple with her tiny hand and a glow of light slowly spread out and the apple grew and ripened right before her eyes until it was big and red and almost too heavy for the branch to bear. Jane reached out and took the apple. She smiled in thanks to the pixie. The pixie returned her smile, waved a tiny hand, and disappeared back into the leaves. Suddenly the voices near the tunnel drew her attention again and she bit deeply into the apple while she listened. Ten Adherents had been left guarding the slaves, and they looked about nervously.

"Where's the last group?" another asked. "They should have met us here by now."

The woods had gone strangely silent around her, as though the whole forest knew something was happening and was expectantly holding its breath, waiting to see who would win the coming battle. Suddenly Jane saw a goblin that almost resembled a tree it was so brown and its skin was as lined and furrowed as bark. He looked at her, nodded, and then stepped out from between the trees where he had been hidden and hooted at the Adherents.

"What's that?"

"One of the slaves slipped his chains," the main voice replied. "You two go bring him back."

Jane watched from her hiding place as the two robed Adherents started towards where the goblin continued to wave at them and laugh. She could see that the Adherents carried something that looked like a gun, but the barrel ended in a cone shape that flared out.

"Get back here you little monster, or we'll shoot," the Adherent shouted at the goblin that finally ducked back under the cover of his trees, and started running to the south. They both broke into a run and suddenly disappeared into the ground as though it opened up and swallowed them. One moment they were on firm ground, and the next a yawning portal in the earth opened up. With a shout of surprise, the men disappeared.

"Bah, look sharp," the leader of the Adherents shouted. "There are more goblins about. Feel free to shoot anything that moves." He pulled his own musket from his back and pulled back the hammer.

Jane was still wondering what the shape of the muskets did when another goblin appeared between the trees and one of the Adherents fired at it. A huge flash of light left the barrel and round ball of glowing energy streaked across the field and slammed into the goblin, knocking him senseless. Suddenly a hundred more goblins began to filter between the trees, and the Adherents began shouting and shooting. A rumble of noise off to her right drew Jane's attention, and she watched in awe as a creature more than twelve feet tall crashed from between the apple trees and ran at the Adherents. There was a volley of three balls of light. All of the shots struck the giant, but it shrugged off the blows and grabbed a robed figure in each hand. It then turned and tossed the Adherents high into the air where they disappeared into the forest after flying hundreds of yards. Moments later the fighting was over, and six unconscious Adherents were being chained together with the chains the goblins had just removed from the long line of former slaves.

"It's finished here," Tasker said suddenly, looking exhilarated and excited as he popped into view next to Jane. "Come on. Let's go recruit." He led her from her hiding place and smiled at her as he did. "You figured it out, didn't you?"

"Yes," Jane muttered shortly. She looked over at the tunnel entrance, which had just reformed back to its original shape. "I could actually see the map in three dimensions," she explained as they walked to where Puck and his goblins were freeing the slaves and seeing to those of their number that had been knocked senseless by the Adherents muskets.

"Gifted," was all Tasker muttered before he stopped in front of the freed slaves and raised his hands for silence.

Jane looked over the group and decided it was a motley assortment of beings if ever she had seen . . . well different creatures. Over half of them were human and looked to be in reasonably decent health. There were a fair number of short beings that she assumed were dwarves, along with a sprinkling of centaurs and bull-headed minotaurs.

"Friends," Tasker cried aloud as the noise and murmurings quieted. "Most of you know who I am. We're going to free those held on the Prison Islands tonight. I beg that you join us. Cain has taken much from all of us, and it's time to start taking some of our lives back from him."

There was a rousing round of agreements that echoed across the clearing, and Jane could tell from the grim faces that this group of freed slaves was going to help no matter what the cost. They were warriors, who had been held in bonds for too long. Now was their time for revenge. They were ready and willing to fight for their freedom.

"Puck has weapons for those who need them. Those of you with other skills can make full use of them," Tasker continued. He motioned to the line of goblins that had now gathered after retrieving some of their downed comrades. The two giants stood nearby looking down curiously at the rest of the collection of beings, trying to watch where they placed their feet. Jane wondered what the trolls would look like, when suddenly she saw a thick-limbed being rambling up from the deeper part of the forest and knew she was looking at trolls. They were shorter than the giants but at least two feet taller than any of the humans, and they carried thick clubs in their hands. Their arms almost dragged on the ground and their skin was the color of mud. As they drew closer, their skin reminded Jane of thick tanned leather. They reminded her of an oversized silverback gorilla only with a thick hide instead of a coat of hair.

"There are two ships yet at the piers and very few guards," Tasker said. "Gather up the remaining robes and magic muskets. We need a group to play the part of the guards. The rest of you gather up your baskets. When this is done, we will have two ships at our disposal. There was a round of muttering as the freed slaves jostled for position. It took longer for them to start moving than Jane thought it would. There was also the matter of finding the keys to the iron manacles and removing them from all their new allies. The sun was sinking low on the horizon when the freed slaves carrying their baskets finally walked down to the beach and started out onto the pier.

"Well, it's about time!"

Jane looked up from where she walked in the middle of the slaves carrying a basket that now contained a small goblin instead of strawberries. She counted twelve more Adherents watching over the last two ships as she walked up the plank following the man in front of her.

"Hey, what are you doing?" echoed a shout as the Adherent tried to bring his musket to bear. His voice was cut off as one of the minotaur grabbed the Adherent and sent him flying off the ship and crashing into the rocks near the pier. There was a round of scuffling as the slaves and hidden goblins overpowered the Adherents, and another round of scuffles when they nearly came to blows on what to do with their new prisoners.

"Tie them up and leave them on the beach," Tasker ordered.

"But they beat us almost every day," muttered a bearded and braided human. He was a barrel-chested man and held the front of an Adherent's black robe tightly in his fist as the unconscious man dangled limply.

"And we won't sink to their level," Tasker repeated. "Let the spirits in the forest deal with them."

The few Adherents who were still conscious paled at the words. Two of them began begging to be taken to the one of the islands and made prisoner there. After a round of laughter, the goblins bound the Adherents hand and foot and left them on the beach in the shadow of the overhanging cliff.

"What will happen to them?" Jane asked Tasker as the ships were made ready and the freed slaves took their place at the oars.

"The spirits in this area are not very forgiving," Tasker muttered. "They've been kept at bay by abominations of machine and magic like these." He pointed down at the stack of captured muskets. "Without their weapons to protect them, the Adherents will not survive mentally and may not survive physically either."

CHAPTER SIXTEEN
The Old Man of Bayfield

JACOB WALKED THE STREETS OF BAYFIELD for the rest of the afternoon, wondering how he was going to get home without resorting to using the iron ring that he had removed from his finger and put in his pocket. He hated the fact that Jane was still there in that other place. He felt he had abandoned her, but he needed to think, and he needed a place to think where life was normal. The sword and shield were stashed under a pile of leaves outside of town and when he decided what to do he would have to hide them in a better place. He was hungry and tired and wanted to sit down and think somewhere for a while.

He realized as he walked that he was more than just hungry. He was famished and after checking his wallet to make sure he had money, he opted for dinner at Maggies. It was only two streets over from where he was standing, and it took him five minutes to make it to the front door. The restaurant was almost empty when he walked in. He sat down at a table near a white-haired man that looked to be in his eighties who was eating alone.

"What can I get you, son?"

Jacob looked up at the waitress and tried to smile but found his thoughts wandering back to Jane and the trouble he had left her in. After a brief look at the menu, he said, "Can I get the all-American burger, fries, and a Mountain Dew?"

The waitress nodded as she took his order, and then a moment later she brought him his drink. "Here you go," she said cheerily. "The burger will be ready in a just few minutes. We're not busy right now."

Jacob nodded and sipped at his drink. *How could I have left Jane. But Tasker lied to us. How could Jane have stayed there?* He argued in his mind as a frown covered his face. He was amazed to find that his strength returned quickly as he drank the sugary liquid. A moment later his glass was empty.

The waitress returned twice to fill his glass, and she gave him an odd look as she filled it the third time. Three minutes later, Jacob stared again at an empty glass. His conscience ate at him. He had abandoned Jane to whatever fate had in store for her and that made him feel miserable.

"Looks like you're carrying the weight of the world on your shoulders, son."

Jacob looked up to see that the older man had pulled his chair over and was looking at him. He was sipping on a cup of coffee and was wearing a pair of jeans and a pull over sweater that was two sizes too large. The sleeves of the sweater came down until they nearly dipped into his coffee.

"It's nothing really," Jacob muttered trying to ignore the old man. *Why can't the old geezer mind his own business?* Jacob thought. To his pleasant surprise, the old man nodded and returned to his own table and once again began sipping coffee and reading his book. When Jacob's food arrived, he dove into it with gusto but found that it didn't taste good at all. It wasn't the food that ruined his meal. It was the fact that Jane's face kept popping up in his mind asking him why he had left her.

Jacob looked out the window. Outside the café, the sun had now set, and Jacob couldn't stop from wondering if the first assault had managed to free any of the slaves. He glanced over at the old man who was calmly flipping pages and read the name on the spine of the book. It was a worn copy of *The*

Hobbit that looked like it had to have been read a hundred times.

"I never get sick of it," the old man said suddenly as his bushy white eyebrows rose up slightly and he looked at Jacob over the top of the book.

"It's not a bad story," Jacob admitted. He had read the book once and thought it was a little slow in the beginning.

"What's wrong, son," the man asked again.

"Why do you think there's something wrong?" Jacob countered as his defenses went up.

"Well, a big kid like you walks in here looking like he is ready to eat a horse, but then when the food arrives he picks at it for thirty minutes," the man said with a fatherly smile. "I raised three boys, and I am not senile. Not yet anyway."

Jacob looked down at his plate and realized the old man was right, his food was pushed around his plate. The burger, picked apart, still had more than a third left and only about half of the fries were gone. His fourth glass of pop was still a third full and most of the ice cubes had melted away. The sweat circle on the table from the glass was beginning to turn into a series of small rivers that drifted across the table as the wood grains rose and fell to the whims of a carpenter from long ago.

"I got lied to recently," he said to the old man almost like the words were pulled from him, "and I got mad and walked away from someone who needed my help," Jacob admitted. "Why is it then that I feel bad? I wasn't the one lying."

"Well," the old man said as he replaced his bookmark. "It's never good to lie to people, but I think it's even worse to abandon those who need our help. Even if you think you have good reason."

"But she told me it was fine if I left," Jacob muttered so loudly that the old man heard every word.

"Sometimes people say things to give those they care about a way to leave even when they want them to stay," the old man said. "I told the same thing to my wife just before she passed. She was holding on just for me. I finally told her to let go, that it was all right for her to leave. Now you tell me—do you think I want her to leave? No! Son, I know this doesn't relate perfectly to what you're saying but the point is still there. I told her go despite wanting her to stay, and she did, she left. Now I won't see her again in this world, but at least I told her how I felt before she left. I bent over and kissed her and told her I'd see her soon. Did you tell her how you felt before you left?"

Jacob pushed his plate aside as he listened to the old man. He wondered what Jane thought of him now. Would she be interested in even speaking to him again? Suddenly he realized the old man was repeating his question.

"Did you tell her how you felt before you left?"

"Huh," Jacob muttered. "Who says there was a girl involved?" he asked defensively.

"Son, the only thing that stands between a growing boy your age and food on the plate in front of him is a girl." The old man laughed.

"No, I didn't," Jacob admitted.

"Is it too late to tell her?" asked the old man.

"I don't know," Jacob said. His mind swirled, he knew he could find Jane again if he wanted to as long as she remained on her map. Would she accept his help? That was a chance he would have to take, but he would take something back to her that would prove he was back for good and that she could trust him. He stood. "But I'm going to find out."

"Good boy," the old man smiled. "You go. I will have the waitress put your meal on my bill."

"Thanks," Jacob said with a smile. He took a last swig of his pop and then headed back out the door and down the street to where his sword and shield were hidden.

It took him five minutes to get back to the spot and he rustled through the leaves until he located the two items. He pulled the shield onto his arm and picked up the sword and its scabbard. Suddenly he heard a rush of footsteps behind and he turned just as a black robed Adherent rushed towards him from across the paved road. He held a wicked looking curved dagger high in the air above his head and a second one in his off hand.

"Get back," Jacob yelled as he raised the shield and intercepted the blow that was directed towards his head. He was nearly skewered by the second knife. "Hey, watch it!" The knife barely missed his arm, but it cut through his sleeve as easily as a razor would have.

"Time to die, boy," the Adherent snarled.

Jacob's eyes went wide. The man truly meant to kill him. He struggled for a moment as he pulled the sword from its sheath and swung it awkwardly at the Adherent. The man leapt back and laughed at him as he struggled to keep his shield and sword in line with his attacker. Jacob was about to step into the Divide when he spotted the small medallion on the man's chest, and he looked down realizing that his ring and medallion were still in his pocket.

"What's the matter, boy," the Adherent said with a smile. "Did you want to go somewhere. Yes, by all means point me straight to your map. My master will enjoy that immensely."

They were standing on the side of the road between two trees when the Adherent attacked again with both knives swinging in a serpent's dance. Jacob felt the shield shudder under multiple hits, and he swung his sword out, hoping that he would strike something that would scare the man enough for him to leave. The moment he began swinging the sword, he had the feeling an ancient spirit worked through him, directing his sword and showing him how hard to parry and when to strike back. The Adherent's eyes went wide, as Jacob began to press him back towards the road. His headlong attack against a young and seemingly inexperienced youth turned into a desperate battle for his own survival. They were in the ditch near the road when Jacob's attention was drawn by another sound.

Suddenly he heard sound of a door closing, and he glanced towards the road. The old man from the restaurant was standing outside his car shouting.

"Get away from the boy," the old man hollered.

The Adherent glanced back and snarled. With a flipping motion of his hand he sent one of his daggers flying end over end at the old man.

"No!" Jacob shouted as the white haired man collapsed against his car clutching at the dagger stuck deep in his shoulder. Something snapped inside Jacob suddenly as he swung his shield hard at the Adherent. The blow struck the knife wielder's hand and sent his other dagger flying. As the man turned to run, Jacob hacked out with the sword's impossibly sharp edge and severed the trunk of a towering oak tree in a single slash. He watched in satisfaction as the oak groaned for a moment and swayed. Then Jacob reached and pushed on the tree, adding the tiniest bit of momentum to the grand tree fall. His aim was perfect, and he smiled when the upper branches fell on the fleeing Adherent and pinned him to the ground.

"Mister, are you all right?" Jacob said as he rushed to where the old man was leaning against his Lincoln town car trying to stop the flow of blood.

"Well, I've been better," the old man said with a smile. "But then I think I see my wife waving to me." He muttered as he closed his eyes and leaned back again the vehicle. There was a smile on his face as he died, and Jacob's eyes filled with tears. He had been so nice. Now here was something that he could truly lay at Cain's feet and not his own. If he had not had a reason before, he had one now that was for certain.

Jacob walked slowly to where the Adherent lay pinned under the tree, the man looked up at him and snarled with an almost inhuman sound.

"Kill me. I don't care," he growled. "You can't stop us."

"Oh, I can at least stop you," Jacob said grimly. Slowly he reached down and tore the man's medallion from his chest, then he walked away as a frightened look filled the Adherent's face. "And I can take your anchor."

"That's it then," the Adherent said as his body began to dissipate. "Doomed to forever walk the Divide. At least I'm free of Cain's power once and for all. You on the other hand will never be free." With those words he completely vanished, leaving only a depression where his body had been.

Jacob slipped his ring from his pocket and slid it onto his hand, and then he stepped into the Divide and searched the maps until he found the one he was looking for. It was there among a dozen others, one that showed in detail the fortress on Madeline Island. He did not enter the map, remembering Tasker's warning about entering a map when he didn't know who owned it. Instead he locked the features in his mind and then went back to Jane's work of art. He chose a spot near where the wall met the lake and stepped through Jane's map and looked around. He would have to be careful how many times he crossed over, but he would bring her news of her sister when he returned, as a peace offering for leaving her.

Behind him the stone wall rose to a uniform height as it followed the lake shore. Ten feet in front of him the waves of Lake Superior rose and fell. He flattened his back to the wall as the sound of footsteps grew close above his head but he breathed a sigh of relief as they continued down the wall. When he was sure that the wall above was empty, he entered and exited the Divide quickly and found that he was perfectly situated just inside the wall and in the deep shadow created by the junction of two walls. The inner courtyard was quiet and filled with shadows. He counted five buildings contained inside the outer wall, and Jacob looked at each of them closely. Of the five he thought only two of them looked like places where a prisoner would be held, so he crept quietly across the gravel yard until he reached the first.

Standing on his toes, he grabbed the ledge of one of the windows and hoisted himself up until he could see inside. There were bars on the window, and he squinted between the bars until he could make out the details of the room. Sleeping on rough cots against the wall were two humans and three short beings that Jacob decided must be dwarves.

"Psst," Jacob hissed. He glanced up and down what he could see of the inside of the room and hoped no one else could hear him. The courtyard was completely empty and so was the wall, so he remained hanging where he was. "Hey, wake up."

He was finally rewarded with movement from one of the cots and a low moan. One of the humans turned over in her bed and looked at him.

"Please don't yell," Jacob begged as she opened her mouth.

"I wasn't going to, but who are you?" she replied quietly. Carefully she rose to her feet and glanced at the door. Then she walked to the window and looked at him.

"My name is Jacob, and I'm looking for a girl named Jackie," Jacob explained. "Have you seen anyone by that name here?" His arms were beginning to cramp as he hung there but he held on for dear life.

"Oh, that poor thing," she said in a whisper. "She was here for a while, but I think they moved her somewhere else because I haven't seen her in a while. She was so terrified when they took her that she barely ate for weeks."

"Blast," Jacob muttered. He shook his head. He should have known it wouldn't be so easy. "How long ago did you see her last?"

"I don't know. Maybe a month," she replied. She looked nervously at the locked door and then back at him. "Look, if they hear us talking, I'll get beaten, and you'll get killed. You should go."

"All right," Jacob said. "Thanks for your help." He dropped to the ground and looked around. The guard who was walking the outer wall was about to make his turn back to this side so he stayed silently crouched in the shadow under the window until he was gone and then moved on to the next building. This one was a bit lower and but the bars on the window were closer together. Opposite the low building was a small structure built of block and sheathed in iron. A thick iron gate protected the only entrance. When he tried to enter it through the Divide, he was rebuffed.

"I didn't know I could be blocked from entering a place on a map," Jacob muttered to himself as he returned to his perch under the barred windows. The attempt left him as tired as though he had run a mile at a sprint, and he leaned against the wall trying to catch his breath. That was something he would definitely have to speak with Tasker about the moment he caught up with Jane and the dwarf.

He risked a glance in the first window and shuddered at what he saw. Chains hung from the ceiling, and two huge creatures that reminded him of minotaurs from the *Chronicles of Narnia* movies were suspended from the ceiling. Neither one moved much when he looked in, but he saw the eyes of one turn to follow him as he left. They would definitely find help here if they came asking for it. The next window was covered from the inside, and he couldn't see anything inside so he moved on to the last window. After waiting for the pacing sentry to pass one more time, he glanced in the window and looked around. This room contained a small office with a thin man sitting at a writing desk bent over a stack of paper.

Jacob pulled his head back just as the man looked over to the window. He ducked low when the man walked over and stared out the window for a minute. When he seemed to have given up on whatever peaked his interest, he walked back to the desk and seated himself again. The man seemed to finishing up whatever he was working on because, a few minutes later, he turned down his lantern and stepped out of the office and left the room closing the door behind him.

"I wonder if he saw me?" Jacob muttered. He glanced through the window again but the office area was now empty. The windows on this room were not barred, and the shutters were open, so he squirmed over sill and tip-toed to the outer door. After listening for any sign of movement from outside the door, he slid it open ever so slightly and looked down the inner hall. It was completely empty except for the doors that exited the hallway on either side at regular intervals.

He turned back to the desk and began looking over the papers stacked on it. Most of them were written in English and seemed to be shipping manifests and destinations. He kept scanning for anything that contained Jackie's name. He was beginning to despair of finding anything when suddenly he spotted the name "Jackie" on a list of prisoners being transferred. He scanned down to the destination and found it was listed as the holding prison at a place called the Isle of Lakes. Carefully he folded the paper and slipped it into his pocket, he was about to leave when the sound of boots on the wooden planks of the floor outside the room drew his attention. Without waiting, he slipped into the Divide and looked about.

CHAPTER SEVENTEEN
Island Hopping

J ANE CROUCHED NEAR THE EDGE of the ships railing looking out at the square watch tower constructed on a rocky knoll that overlooked the only sheltered spot on this side of the island. Along the railing were crouched nearly a hundred of Puck's goblins and around twenty of the freed slaves. Thankfully Puck's forces each had carried four or five weapons apiece and the extra swords and daggers were quickly passed out among the freed slaves.

More importantly the captured Adherent firearms and uniforms were prominently displayed on eight volunteers who stood imperiously on the ships aft deck and looked down at the rowers. Hidden with the others at the front of the ship were eight more freed slaves carrying eight more muskets primed and ready to fire.

"It's about time ye got back!"

Bella narrowed her eyes as she peeked out for a moment and counted the awaiting Adherents, all low-ranking members of the organization, little more than bullies, dangerous only when armed. They swaggered up and down the beach with their muskets slung over their shoulders seeming not in the least concerned that their fellows were an hour late and riding much lower in the water than normal.

"Hurry up. We're getting hungry, and the rest of the trash is getting restless."

Jane risked a glance from behind a barrel stacked on the deck. Before her she saw the speaker was a short swarthy dwarf who carried a musket twice his height. Still, despite the size of the weapon, the dwarf's gnarled hands held it easily, showing his great strength. His bulbous nose shook as he berated the men guarding the ship. She glanced back as two of the rowers leapt up and tossed mooring lines across the gap between the ship and the pier. When the ship was tied off, there was a muffled shout, and eight musket wielders rose and fired almost at once. A volley of energy crackled across the space between the ship and the beach, and fully half the defenders fell down unconscious before they knew what was happening. Amazingly the boisterous dwarf still stood, his eyes almost disappearing into his bushy eyebrows. He fumbled with his musket, trying to line up a shot, but suddenly he dropped his musket and howled in pain.

"Take that!" Bella shouted in a small voice that was almost lost as the forces aboard the ship stormed ashore. Her small bow hummed as she released another arrow and again struck the dwarf in the tip of his protruding nose, drawing another howl of pain. Then his cries were silenced as a human and an elf knocked him to the ground and roped his arms and feet together.

Suddenly Jane realized that the battle, barely begun, was over and she was still clutching the railing in a white-knuckled grip. A rousing round of cheers broke out across the beach as the freed slaves rushed to meet loved ones who remained on the island while they were sent to work.

"It's part of how the Adherents control people," Bella said in a small voice, having flown back to Jane. "They separate those sent to work from their loved ones to make sure they come back."

"Who's going to run away when they can take out their revenge on those who are left behind?" Jane reasoned as she walked to where the gangplank was resting on the rock. The plank creaked loudly as she crossed, and she whispered a prayer when she finally stood on dry land again.

"So it begins," Tasker said with a grim smile. "I already sent a group to the far side of the island to take the group of Adherents there. We can't afford to lose any of the ships from here out, if any of them slip free and make it to Madeline Island to warn the garrison, we'll face more than we can handle."

"How many Adherents are stationed there?" Jane asked again.

"A small army," Tasker admitted. "Without Jacob to scout for us, we must assume that there are maybe a thousand at most but five hundred at the least." He looked over at the group of prisoners huddled on the beach and narrowed his eyes at the small dwarf. "I knew him once. His mother lived in Duluth near one of the deep mines. He used to play with neighborhood kids. He even brought me trinkets in exchange for stories from the old days." Tasker shook his head as the dwarf turned his pleading eyes towards him.

"What will we do with them?" Jane asked.

"Leave them here without a boat," Tasker said simply. "Not a one of them can swim well enough with this cold water to make it to shore. They won't starve but it won't be easy for them either. We'll return later to pass judgment, but this night is for freeing loved ones."

Jane breathed a sigh of relief. There was a different code in this world, but she had hoped they wouldn't try to harm the helpless despite what they had been once.

"It's time for us to move," Tasker said. "We still have much to do this night." He looked up at the moon, which was just beginning its nightly journey through the sky. It took an hour for the group sent to the far side of the island to return with the ship that had docked there, giving them a total of four ships now and nearly twenty-five of the muskets. Tasker motioned for silence, and finally the mutterings came to a halt.

"Puck, the battle has just begun, but we must already divide out forces if we are to win this night," Tasker said loudly. He unrolled his map and motioned to those around him. "We stand on Rocky Island right now. To our east is South Twin Island and to our south is Otter Island. We'll send two ships to each island. Their ships already docked at those places must be taken intact. I mean to take all the islands north of Stockton and Oak Islands this night . . ."

A round of muttering swelled, and he held up his hand. "With the exception of Bear Island. That situation must be handled on another night." Now nods around the small fire that now lit the beach confirmed that Bear Island was a dangerous place. "It's vital we take the ships. Remember, without enough ships, the assault on Madeline Island can't happen, and that will leave a strong force of enemy soldiers within easy striking distance of our recent gains."

Puck nodded.

"To the ships!" Tasker cried in a loud voice. "You stick with me, girl. We're going south."

Jane nodded and followed the dwarf as he hurried towards the ship they had just left such a short time ago. They arranged their forces in a similar manner for the second assault, and Jane was happy to find only a single guard post built on Otter Island. The twenty or so Adherents standing guard over the hundred or so inhabitants of Otter Island were completely unprepared for an lake assault, and most were unconscious before the ship was even tied to the pier. Most of the prisoners on Otter Island were spouses and children of those already freed and they ran to greet their loved ones with great smiles on their faces and squeals of joy.

"We must keep moving," Tasker urged as he tried to regain the attention of those still locked in fierce embraces with their long-lost spouses. Still it took nearly an hour before his forces were back aboard all three ships—the two he came with and the one he had just captured—and the long oars were pushing them towards the imposing black mass that was Manitou Island.

Jane looked out from her hiding place and noticed that this time the beach was clear of Adherents. A few fires burned untended with their cooking pots. "They know something's wrong," she muttered. She turned towards Tasker and motioned to her map with a questioning look in her eyes.

"Not yet, girl," Tasker replied from where he stood behind a human dressed in Adherent robes and holding his musket ready. "Word is beginning to spread, but right now it's simply a group of slaves who've gotten control of a ship and are causing problems. When we start using our magic, it'll show anyone with talent who's watching. If only Jacob were here, he could slip through unnoticed and find out where they're waiting. Also your last lesson on the map will come just before we strike at Madeline Island, and it will be your last test. If you pass it, we'll win the day. But if you fail, we'll lose and be run off like so much rabble on the waves."

They were within a hundred yards of the shore when a volley of shots rang out, and nearly twenty musket shots raked across the deck of the lead ship. Half a dozen solders fell to the deck, but others pressed forward and made ready to leap onto the shore. This time the beach was littered with unconscious rebels by time the island was secured, and nearly thirty Adherents were trussed tightly together in a group inside one of the very stockades they used to separate the slaves. Two ships had been docked at this island, and both of them were taken with minor scuffles with the watchers who seemed to have withdrawn to their barriers on shore and trusted in their muskets to carry the battle.

The night was waning when they landed on an unwatched section of the shore of Oak Island, and Tasker sent half of his forces overland while the rest pulled hard at the oars and swung the ship around to the other side of the island. There were four ships tied to the piers on the northern tip of Oak Island, and as they approached, one of the ships cut free of its moorings and made for the open water.

"Go stop them!" Tasker shouted to the closest vessel. "Sink it if you must but stop them!"

The bearded human nodded and swung the rudder of his ship about, the banks of oars on his ship dug deeply into the lake water as they strove to close the distance.

Jane watched for a time, and then brought her attention back to the structures on the rocky overhang that watched over Oak Island. A rough stockade had been built atop a bluff. From the shouts and flashes of light, she decided the forces they had landed earlier must have engaged the guards.

"There are two armories north of Madeline Island," Tasker explained as the ship they were on pulled close to the rocky cliff underneath the stockade, and at least fifty of the smaller goblins leapt over the side and started up the rocky cliff. When the climbers were away, they moved the ship in next to the pier and made it fast at the moorings. The other vessels were unguarded and soon appropriated. That brought their flotilla to nine. "Also in the past there were close to a thousand slave kept here and almost two hundred soldiers." There were shouts and taunts that echoed off the rocks as the slaves attacking from the front of the stockade met with heavy resistance. The soldiers here were well-armed and more than just bullies. These were trained soldiers and well-versed at using the muskets they all carried.

Jane could see unconscious forms scattered about the front of the fortifications, and the few shots still fired from the tree line seemed to going wild. "What are they doing?"

"They're giving us a chance to get into position without being seen," Tasker replied. He led his band of about a hundred up the ramp that led to the southern side of the stockade. They reached the wooden barricade unseen. "And it gives the trolls a chance to remove these logs from our way." Tasker motioned the tall creatures forward and watched as the long-armed creatures ambled closer.

Jane watched in amazement as the trolls grasped the logs and pulled with all their might. At first the timbers resisted but then slowly they gave way and broke with a resounding snap. The sound went unnoticed from the inside. When three more logs had been removed, Tasker nodded and led his force through the gap and into the stockade. Jane followed at the back of the group, not wanting to get in the way of those who were fighting. There were shouts of surprise as the Adherents guarding the walls were suddenly set upon from behind. Shouts of derision aimed at those outside the walls suddenly turned to cries of alarm. Fights broke out across the platform built into the timber wall, and then the forces outside rushed forward again pressing to join their comrades. This time knives and sword flashed in the light of the torches, and Jane turned away not wanting to see what was happening.

There were two buildings inside the stockade, and Jane made her way towards the smaller of the two. Iron bars stretched across the window, but she slid the door open carefully not sure what she would find. When she heard nothing, she entered and looked around. Inside she saw six bunks build into the walls. The blankets had been thrown off them in what looked like hurried departures. There was a wooden door with three iron bands crossing the middle. It hung ajar. From down the hall behind the door, Jane heard shouts and cries for help. She grabbed a sturdy cudgel from atop a table and walked quietly to the door.

Down the hall she could see two Adherents. One removed a thick set of keys from his belt and worked the lock on one of the cells. From inside the cell echoed a desperate cry for help as whoever was held in the cell rattled the door and tried to stop them from entering. It was a woman's voice and turned to pleading when the door finally swung open and the first of the Adherents entered the room.

"Time to go. Cain's doesn't want one of his best prizes to be lost to him. I think we'll slip away into the lake and let the garrison at Madeline Island handle these rabble rousers."

Jane walked quietly down the hall to where the other Adherent was leering into the cell, oblivious to what was happening around them.

"Those slaves think they're going to escape, but the master is going to hear of this. When he does, he'll send his forces to wipe this place clean once and for all."

Jane drew back with her club and swung with all her might at the Adherent standing in the door. There was a thud as the cudgel rebounded off his head, and he fell to the floor with a crash.

"What?"

The other Adherent emerged from the cell dragging a willowy elfin woman clothed in what had probably been at one time a fine gown. Now it was ripped and torn in many places and covered in filthy stains. Still she tried to struggle against the brutish man as he looked up in surprise at Jane.

"How dare you!" he shouted as he dropped the woman's arm and shoved her back into the cell.

Jane swung the club as hard as she could again, but this time the Adherent caught the descending club in his hand. There was a loud smacking sound as his beefy hand intercepted the wood and turned it to the side. With a grunt, he tore the cudgel from her hands and threw it off to the side. From his belt he drew a wicked-looking curved dagger and smiled at her.

"I'm going to cut you up, girl."

Jane stumbled backwards but tripped on the inert body on the floor and fell backwards to the ground as she struggled to get away. Then he was standing over her and leaning down with the dagger, smiling. Jane closed her eyes and began to pray as hard as she could that something or someone had seen her enter the building and would come to her aid. She felt the rough hands grab her hair and yank her head back and she beat her fists on the iron muscles of the brute's arm to no avail.

CHAPTER EIGHTEEN
Four Princesses

W HAT?"
The brute suddenly released his grip on her, and Jane fell heavily to the floor. When she opened her eyes she saw a long sword resting lightly on the Adherent's neck, and a thin line of blood running down the man's robes.

"If you want to live," Jacob said slowly. "You'll drop the knife and slowly hand the keys that unlock these shackles to my friend here."

The Adherent released his grip on the knife, and it clattered to the floor. Then he carefully removed the thick ring of keys from his belt and handed them to Jane.

"You came back," Jane said with a wide smile. Her voice quavered as relief flooded through her. She could have kissed him right then and there.

"I met an old man who helped me see the light," Jacob said. "I'm sorry I left you. Let's chain these two up and see how my newest friend here is fairing." He pulled his head towards the sturdy cell behind them and the fine features of the elfin woman once again appeared in the door. "This is Eriunia one of the four princesses of the Tuatha De Danann."

Jacob struggled through the words as he kept the sword tightly against the Adherent's neck. There was murder in the black-robed man's eyes, and Jane decided it would be best to lock him up before continuing the conversation. Thankfully Jacob was of the same mind and motioned with his shield toward a cell.

"Into the cell, Adherent," Jacob ordered. When the man was completely through the door he kicked him hard in the butt and sent him flying forward into the wall while he stepped back, and Eriunia slammed the door shut. Moments later the lock clicked into place and they all breathed a sigh of relief.

"I'm pleased to meet you," Eriunia said with a graceful bow to Jane. She smiled and held out her hand. "If you would be so kind as to free my hands while Jacob deals with this other cretin, we can discuss our current state of affairs without this accursed iron."

Jane's eyes narrowed in a brief surge of jealousy as she saw Jacob smile at the young prisoner and then immediately rush to open another cell and pull the still unconscious Adherent into it. She shook away the feelings and fumbled with the keys until she found the right one. The iron shackles fell to the floor. Jane felt shame and embarrassment rise up in her as she thought about how dirty and worn she felt but how, despite the tattered state of her clothes, Eriunia still looked like a queen and moved with perfect grace.

"He's locked up," Jacob said after a moment. He looked at Jane and sighed, "I'm sorry I ran. Can you forgive me?" His head dipped and he kicked the floor with his foot as he slipped his sword back into its sheath. "I was just . . . I really missed you . . ." His words were cut off as Jane wrapped her arms around his neck and looked deeply into his eyes. She kissed him once long and hard and then smiled as she took a step back.

"What was that for?" Jacob asked. "Not that I'm complaining of course."

"That's for coming back when you did," Jane said with a breathless smile. "Although, Jacob, I'm thinking about slapping you for leaving me when you did."

"Before you do that, hear me out," Jacob said. He raised his hands defensively before her. "Before I returned here I visited Madeline Island on our side of the Divide. I know what the fortress there looks like and where its weakest points are. Even more, I know where the prisoners are being held."

Jane's eyes widened as her hand flew to her mouth, "Is she there?" Her eyes fell again a moment later as Jacob shook his head.

"I'm sorry, no," Jacob replied. "But I think I have an idea of where she is." He pulled out the folded paper and showed it to her. "It was the only thing that had her name on it. We just have to find out where this Isle of Lakes is."

Eriunia had taken the keys from Jane was opening cell doors when she heard them say the name and she nearly dropped the keys. "That's a place of much evil," she said in a quiet voice. There were seven others being held in the small cells and four of them were kin of Eriunia's people. Despite their haggard condition they held themselves proudly and walked gracefully to the front door of the building. Tasker was leading his band of fighters towards the building when Jacob and Jane emerged leading Eriunia and the others. A wide smile broke on his face when he saw them.

"Back together," Tasker said happily. "I just spoke with Puck, and he's captured the Outer Island and will land his forces on Stockton Island where we'll join him." The day was brightening now quickly, and Jane squirmed uncomfortably. She noticed Tasker looking at her, and he nodded with a hesitant look on his face.

"What is it?"

"It's my sister," Jane said in a broken voice. "She was here but was sent to some place called the Isle of Lakes. Do you know where that is?"

Tasker's face fell as he nodded, "I know of the place."

"Where?" Jane pressed. "Where is she?"

"It is the gateway to those being sent to the northern iron mines," Tasker explained. He led them into the small prison building and unrolled his map on the table there. "Here along the northern shores of Lake Superior. I believe it's marked as Isle Royale in your world. Outside of Manitoulin Island, it contains the largest concentration of Adherent forces in the entire Five Lakes Territories."

"How many?" Jane asked as her heart fell.

"At least five thousand," Bella replied before Tasker could. "Almost the entire island is fortified, and it's the home port for twenty of the great iron warships that Cain's built."

"It is impossible then, isn't it?" Jane muttered as she slumped to the crude chair that stood near the table. "I just want to see her again."

"No it isn't," Tasker replied. "But we have to break his power here first. Then his forces on Manitoulin Island will be cut off and we will find a way to break them. One battle at a time."

"I do know that there's something of great value on Madeline Island," Jacob broke in finally. He looked around and made sure he caught everyone's eyes before he continued. "When I was searching through the fortress there, I found an iron gate built into a block building that I couldn't break through. Not even from inside the Divide. It seemed to be outside my reach. The entire building was sheathed in iron and it felt cold to the touch. I tried to pass through the Divide and enter it and I couldn't."

"Cold iron it is the bane of magical folk everywhere. You may think of iron as just a material for building and making things in your world, but it has many properties that have been forgotten across the Divide," Tasker muttered. "I did not even know such a thing was possible." *Still where better to hide a thing that needed to be protected at all costs,* Tasker thought. "Where better to store a dragon's egg than inside a building of cold iron that would rebuff even a dragon's attempt to regain it. If we take Madeline Island, we'll need have the services of Yerdarva the red, and we'll make Cain pay for what he's done."

When Tasker stopped speaking, Eriunia rose and motioned for silence. "As one of the four princesses of the Tuatha De Danann, I speak a word of warning to all present. This Cain has become more than just a local problem. He has made deals with many around the world and the words of his Temple of Adherency are even now spreading far and wide. There have been book burnings in the Emerald Isle, in the desert reaches of Nubia and across the great steppes of China. Battles have been fought in many places, and this is but one part of a great struggle that threatens to tear our world asunder."

"What would you have us do, elf?" asked a bearded human who had been one of the first freed. "Give up and die? We have no further retreat to call our own as do those of the Tuatha De Danann."

"Nay, never give up," Eriunia said fiercely. "Never surrender, for hope still burns while yet one remains free."

"Will the denizens of Tuatha De Danann lend us aid?" another asked hopefully.

"This Cain has a long reach and his Adherents have been sent far and wide," Eriunia said sadly. "When the four princesses of the Tuatha De Danann were kidnapped, the passage between our world and yours was closed. None will pass that way until the four are returned. Then Cain knows that the might of the elf people will descend on this world with every weapon both magical and mundane that they can muster.

However, until the four are safe, those that are here are cut off from their homes."

"It's our responsibility to turn the tide here and begin the destruction of the Temple of Adherency," Tasker said fervently. "We begin what we may never finish, but we'll make ourselves heard over the burning of books and the shouts of those who would remake the world into their image."

They all left the building and walked slowly down to where the freed slaves were securing the ships for the night and rounding up the prisoners and putting the Adherents who had survived into their own holding cells. The sun was rising and the warmth of the day made Jane yawn loudly.

"Tasker . . ." she started, but he waved his hand.

"Go to your world both of you," Tasker said. "We will spend this day and tomorrow rounding up those left on these islands. When you return, we'll strike at Madeline Island, but you should reassure your loved ones and prepare a good story for your next absence."

Jane smiled and hugged the short man.

"We'll find your sister, Jane," Tasker muttered when she finally released her grip on him. "That I promise."

The End of Book One

Epilogue

Tasker watched as Jane and Jacob faded from view and traversed through the Divide back to their world. The moment they were gone his shoulders slumped and he walked slowly to where he could look done at the small flotilla tied off to the docks. He was tired and unsuredespite the advances they had managed in less then three days. So far the fledgling revolt had control of at least nine wooden cargo ships and maybe double that number would be added when the forces that Puck had landed on the far side of the island made their way here.

"Wooden cargo ships against Ironships built for war," Tasker muttered. "We will have to plan carefully." Still he thought we have gathered at least two thousand able bodied warriors and more would come as the Prison Islands were liberated and those who refused to bend the knee to the Temple came to join them. It was further then he had made it the last time, but he dared not dwell on those thoughts. This time was different, Jane was a gifted Map Maker and Jacob had learned the Runners ways quickly.

"What is wrong Tasker?" Bella said as she floated up beside him on the wall. Her face was glowing but that was the way with Fairies, forever looking forward.

"Nothing really," Tasker replied. "We have the beginnings of a great movement here. I was just considering how best to take advantage of our gains."

"What if Cain finds out what is happening and sends his fleets and armies out?" Bella asked in a quiet voice.

"Then we fade back into the wilderness and continue to strike when we are able." Tasker hardened his resolve and shrugged off the dark feelings. "We will regain Yerdarva's egg and add her might to ours; we will find Jane's sister and set her free. I will not sit by idly while Cain desecrates our world under a banner that I once thought would bring better lives to everyone on this side of the Divide."

They stood looking down as the night watch took its place both on the ships and across the wooden walls of the stockade. Vigilance was required now lest word of their progress find its way across the great lake and down into Lake Huron where Cain's forces were heavily concentrated. As Tasker turned to leave his spot on the wall, he thought about phrase he had heard while wandering the other side searching for Jane.

He had stood silently in front of what the humans across the Divide called a television set and listened intently as the picture in the glass spoke and these words had haunted him.

"One ought never to turn one's back on a threatened danger and try to run away from it. If you do that, you will double the danger. But if you meet it promptly and without flinching, you will reduce the danger by half. Never run away from anything. Never!"

Long after the words had stopped Tasker stood thinking about them and what they had tried each time Cain came to them. They turned their backs, packed up their things, and quietly left. Each time they believed what Cain said, each time they hoped they would be left alone and each time their mistakes had followed them.

"Here," Tasker muttered under his breath. "Here is where we stop running; here is where we will meet him without flinching." Tasker alone believed he knew what Cain was searching for and if he found it their world would never be safe every again.

Coming Soon

The Map Maker's Sister